Sixteen
YEARS
OF
DUST

Sixteen YEARS OF DUST

Stories of Civil War

HAAS H MROUE

SIXTEEN YEARS OF DUST
STORIES OF CIVIL WAR

iUniverse books may be ordered through booksellers or by contacting:

iUniverse
1663 Liberty Drive
Bloomington, IN 47403
www.iuniverse.com
1-800-Authors (1-800-288-4677)

ISBN: 978-1-5320-3411-4 (sc)
ISBN: 978-1-5320-3410-7 (e)

Library of Congress Control Number: 2017915038

Print information available on the last page.

iUniverse rev. date: 11/07/2017

Contents

Contents

Other Books by Haas Mroue

Beirut Seizures
The Passport Stamper
Cucumber & Mint
A Photojournalist, Kabul to Beirut
Amsterdam Day by Day
Memorable Walks in Paris

Foreword

'We lived a war with no name
and escaped. We now belong to a culture
That has no name.'[1]

In these eight short stories of Haas Mroue we are given some of the most haunting and evocative conjurings of Lebanon under the turmoil of its sixteen-year Civil War.

Haas was born and raised in Beirut. In 1975, when he was ten, he and his mother fled the war and their homeland. All of Haas's writings are deeply informed by this uprooting. The Lebanese Civil war becomes not just the backdrop for his fiction but is in its own way the central character. The conflict-ravaged country informs the psyche of the characters. Like a traumatised mother that cannot be there for her children, she leaves her child longing for something illusory - a stable, pre-war land, a connection and a rootedness that can never be obtained because the reality is just instability and violence. And yet still the search is for this ideal, an end to the fighting, an end to war. It becomes a central quest in all of Haas's work - what responsibility are each of us willing to take on, to stop the wars once and for all?

The first six stories that make up this collection of stories represent Haas's fictional writings that directly relate to the fighting that ravaged his country between 1975 and 1991. In a kaleidoscope of haunting imagery the different characters and perspectives work together to build up a wide panorama, full of breathtaking detail. It offers those of us to whom this is another world an astonishingly vivid picture and understanding. And to those who have lived through it, all those 'Beirut Survivors', those who, in Haas's words, you can see in their eyes have been to Beirut, to them the stories are frighteningly real and personal.

The stories were written at various points throughout Haas's life, when he was living in London, Paris, and latterly the USA. Alongside his fictional writing and poetry he was regularly writing for travel guides such as Frommer's, Berlitz, and Lonely Planet, and working as editor of Airways Magazine. This constant movement and searching is reflected in the stories and informed by the many Lebanese Haas met who, like him, had fled the war and their homeland and were now scattered around the world. 'Where do we belong but to the memories?'[2] Those who have escaped are still defined by what they have run from.

The first story in this collection, "The Sea of Yellow Mud", looks at the causes of war as a nine year old would understand them. It is a fictionalised autobiography of Haas's own experience of evacuation, leaving behind his best friend, his dog Snoopy. It speaks powerfully of the influence of the political on the everyday.

In "Cucumber and Mint" we see a mother forced into making the drastic choice of leaving her home and country. In Lebanon, the role of head of household often falls to the mother, as the husband is off seeking employment in one of the neighbouring wealthy Gulf states. In a time of war the mother's responsibility suddenly extends beyond the day-to-day to those decisions with a massive life-changing consequence.

'Civil War' asks the question of what it means to be a man. In a land of absent fathers, taken by work or by war, there is no role model to follow. And often if the father has fallen in battle the boy feels obligated to fight himself, out of some sort allegiance, some need for connection. In this story we see a boy seduced by the idea of fighting, but confronted by the reality of it. Haas's own father, Professor Hassib Mroue died three months before Haas was born, at the tragically young age of thirty-six. His mother brought him up as a single parent. Part of Haas's longing and connection for Lebanon can perhaps be explained because it is the land in which his unknown father lies.

'Beyond the Horizon' is based on the true-life case of Amoulaki, a Lebanese woman, torn between emigrating or not. It demonstrates the emotional cost of the war. Behind the external stability and support of family and a good income, the trauma of the civil war has lodged itself somewhere within her and will come out one way or another.

The fifth story in the collection is 'A Sunday in Beirut.' It conjures up the mundanity of life, an everyday Sunday, but set against the extraordinary backdrop of a country destroying itself. It is a juxtaposition extremely powerful in its simplicity.

The title story shows people's various coping strategies in terms of how to deal with a war-torn home. 'Sixteen Years of Dust' is centred at the Cannes Film Festival, which Haas visited a number of times during the eighties when he was a student in Paris. Here Haas tells the story of how some Lebanese who have fled the conflict have cut themselves off from their homeland and its people. To them the civil war and the human cost are merely a commodity - something to exploit for material gain and personal fame. In this story the loss of a sister, whose death in a red VW we have already encountered in 'Civil War', becomes the subject of a film. War offers a tidy profit for those dissociated enough from the true cost.

Running on Wind takes us to another country and another struggle, with the story of a Palestinian refugee who is always running from war. She has fled from the conflict in her own land and is then forced to flee again when the Lebanese refugee camps in Tyre come under attack. She is now in Kuwait with her husband and another war has caught up with her.

The final story of the collection, 'Occupation Photojournalist', is one of Haas's earliest published stories and it won him an award when he was studying at the University of Paris in 1984. It is a haunting, abstract story set in a nameless country in the grip of famine. 'After war there is famine and more death'[3]. Though not set in or directly related to Lebanon, it is a story that could only have been written by Haas and is deeply informed by his experiences. It was a theme Haas has to return to in a screenplay, when he brought it closer to home. In 'A Photojournalist: Kabul to Beirut' he explores further how 'The wars just go on and on and we keep taking photographs.'[4] The screenplay has recently been published for the first time and makes for a powerful and pertinent read.

Alongside the stories, this book also features a couple of personal commentaries by two of Haas's close friends, Joseph Trad and Sana Chebaro. And there is a haunting epilogue "Once Upon a Time" by Haas's mother Najwa Mounla, that grapples with the trauma of loss through the power of writing. Finally there is a glossary explaining Lebanese words and locations.

In 2007 Haas returned to Beirut. Surrounded by extended family and friends and in the landscape that formed him, he wrote how at last he felt he had truly become his father's son. Whilst on that trip, in the bosom of his homeland, Haas tragically suffered a massive heart attack and died suddenly at the shockingly young age of forty-one.

Haas was one of the most original and poetic voices to come out of the political turmoil of Lebanon and it seems a timely moment to bring his stories to a wider audience. Most of Lebanon's land border is with Syria, whose troubles are never far from our front pages. It is estimated that Syrian refugees fleeing across the border to escape now make up over a quarter of Lebanon's population. The refugee crisis shows no sign of abating, calling on all of us in the west to face up to our responsibilities to our fellow citizens, to recognise our common humanity. When the wars have no name, we can finally see that it is just the same story again and again, endlessly repeating, and that we are all one.

Children and birds suffer most in war.
(...) Children and birds are always running away.[5]

Simon Lys
2015

Simon Lys is a playwright and short story writer. He feels a deep connection with Haas's work and has been honoured to work closely with Haas's mother Najwa Mounla in preparing Haas's unpublished work for publication.

---

[1] Beirut Survivors Anonymous by Haas H. Mroue - Beirut Seizures (2nd Edition, iUniverse 2012)

[2] Beirut Survivors Anonymous II by Haas H. Mroue - Beirut Seizures (2nd Edition, iUniverse 2012)

[3] Migration by Haas H. Mroue - Beirut Seizures (2nd Edition, iUniverse 2012)

[4] A Photojournalist : Kabul to Beirut by Haas Hassib Mroue (Authorhouse 2015)

[5] Migration by Haas H. Mroue - Beirut Seizures (2nd Edition, iUniverse 2012)

The Sea of Yellow Mud

Waiting for the elevator, her keys ringing
in the dark corridor, she sighs. Hadi,
his mouth open, sleeping
safe under his blanket. She will put her head
next to his on the pillow
and forget the war.

Haas Mroue, *'While Hadi Sleeps'*

The Sea of Yellow Mud

It was an evening in April. It was the day before the war began. Guy sat in a bathtub full of bubbles, playing with his toy cars. Outside the *Khamsin* blew softly from the South. Snoopy, Guy's beagle, sat on the bathroom tiles cocking his ears. "Vroom, vroom, vroom!" Guy slid his cars along the side of the tub. It was a Thursday night. He was eight years old.

"Guy, tomorrow's a school day, hurry up." His mother walked into the bathroom, holding out a yellow towel for him. She was going out after he fell asleep. She had been humming to herself all afternoon. Guy dried himself with his towel. His mother handed him a Q-Tip.

"Mom, are we going skiing Saturday?" Guy asked, smelling the used Q-Tip. "If there's enough snow," she said, drying his hair. "This warm wind is melting it all."

That night, before Guy fell asleep, he prayed the snow would not melt before the weekend. Snoopy slept at his feet. The walls of Guy's room were lined with posters of skiers and dogs. Everything else was yellow. Even his ski boots under his bed had yellow stickers on them. Guy thought the color yellow made the next day come quicker. He thought yellow made dreams come true.

The sunshine was filtering through the yellow curtains when Guy woke up and glanced at his radio-clock. It flashed 8:00 - 8:00 - 8:00. He ran into the living room, Snoopy at his heels. "Mom!" He screamed. "Why didn't you wake me up? I missed my school bus."

His mother sat on the couch, wearing the red and white bathrobe she wore every morning. She was listening to the news.

"Guy, come here," she said, "there's no school today."

Guy sat down next to her. "Why Mom?"

The newscaster on the radio was talking in a funny way. He was talking quickly.

"Shhh." His mother put her finger to her lips.

Guy did not understand what the newscaster was saying. He thought he heard the words 'dead' and 'machine guns'.

"Come on Snoopy, let's go make pancakes."

Guy and Snoopy fiddled around in the kitchen all morning. Guy's mother sat in the living room, switching stations on the radio. She did not scold him for dripping batter all over the kitchen counter. She did not tell him anything. She was acting funny, Guy thought.

Guy gave Snoopy a bath. He whispered in his ear as he lathered his head. "Whoosh, whoosh, we'll go down the mountain Snoopy. We'll go skiing me and you, okay?"

Guy and Snoopy, both wet, walked back into the living room and sat down on the couch.

"Mom, can I go over to Ray's house and play?"

"We can't go outside today," his mother said. "The streets are not safe."

"But why?" Guy was getting impatient. It was starting to feel like one of those Saturday afternoons when his mother had promised to take him to the movies but then changed her mind because she had stomach pains.

"There are people fighting," his mother said, "and until they stop fighting and put their guns away we have to stay indoors." She played with his wet hair. Guy pushed her hand away.

"But I want to play outside. I'm bored."

"Why don't you read your book?"

"No. I'm bored of reading."

"Then why don't you go blow dry Snoopy's hair."

Guy stormed out of the living room. "You always give me these stupid ideas. I hate your ideas!" he shouted from his bedroom.

He spent the rest of the day teasing Snoopy, putting cookies on the dog's nose, while Snoopy salivated, not getting the cookies until Guy collapsed on his bed in the late evening.

The next day his mother helped him bake a cake. Then Guy drew a picture using his yellow crayons.

"That's Dad when he was as old as me. And that's his dog Blackie," Guy told his mother when she asked him about the drawing. "Grandpa told me that Blackie would follow Dad all the way to school. When's Grandpa coming to visit?"

They were sitting in the kitchen. The cake was cooling by the window. The Khamsin had died down and the air had turned cool and humid.

"Grandpa can't come and visit until the roads are safe," his mother told him.

"And we're not going skiing tomorrow are we?" Guy said. The whole week was turning out to be one long Saturday afternoon.

"No. We can't," said his mother cleaning the kitchen counter with a wet sponge and liquid soap.

"And when can I go to school again?"

His mother walked over to him and sat on a chair beside him.

"Guy, I don't know. Nobody knows, I can't answer all your questions anymore. I wish I knew all the answers. But I don't."

His mother was squeezing the wet sponge without knowing it and Guy watched as the soap dripped from it onto the kitchen table.

By the middle of the second week, the roads were safe again and Guy was able to go to school. His school was in the hills in the suburbs of the city. On his way, Guy saw soldiers holding machine guns.

Sometime these soldiers stopped the school bus and came on board and looked around. Guy and his best friend, Ray, talked about skiing as the soldiers walked up and down the aisle of the bus.

"My mother said that this will be the last weekend of skiing," Ray told Guy, "she said we will go up to the mountains tonight and come back on Sunday."

"We're going up tomorrow too," Guy said.

The sun was strong even so late in the afternoon. The soldiers wore sunglasses. The soldiers got off the bus and waved them on. Ray and Guy arranged to meet the next day on the slopes.

When Guy got home that afternoon he found his mother watching the news on television. She did not hug him. She did not ask him if he was hungry. She opened the door for him and quickly went back to watching TV. Snoopy jumped on Guy. Guy sat next to his mother and watched with her. He saw an elevator and blood around it. He saw a black plastic bag being hauled into an ambulance. His mother began to cry.

"What Mom?" Guy said. "What?" He could sense this was bad. Very bad.

His mother got up and went into the bathroom. She did not close the door. "You know Ray's Dad was in the government before he died?" she asked. Her voice was thicker, heavier.

"Yeah," Guy said. He was standing by the bathroom door, watching his mother wash her face.

"He had lots of enemies and today they killed Ray's Mom."

Guy had never seen his mother cry before. Guy felt something move inside his stomach. He felt the Pepsi he drunk on the bus rising to his throat.

"But you're supposed to call her to figure out about skiing tomorrow," Guy said. "We're going skiing, right?"

His mother did not answer. She was crying again.

That night Guy dreamt that he was on the bus coming home from school. The bus ride was very long. He was thirsty and afraid. Men with machine guns were riding on top of the bus, they were clinging to the sides. Men with machine guns were everywhere. When he got home the elevator was dripping blood and his mother wasn't home. He called out to her and she did not answer. He called for a very long time.

He was shaking when he woke up and ran to his mother's bedroom. He sat on her bed until he could hear her steady breathing. He touched her foot and she woke up.

"What's the matter Guy?"

"I want to sit here, that's all."

She gave him part of her blanket and they sat listening to the wind blowing between the buildings.

"Mom, will they put Ray in one of those big houses for kids that don't have Moms and Dads?" Guy asked.

"You mean an orphanage? No, Ray will stay with his grandparents. I'm sure he is with them right now. We'll call him tomorrow, okay?"

Guy slept on his mother's bed. Before the sun came up Guy was woken up by the strange noises. Thud, thud, thud far away. He could not go to school again and he spent the week playing with his toy cars. Each night the noises got louder and louder. The days passed slowly. Guy missed his room in the cabin in the mountains. He wanted to ski for the last time and one day he wore his ski boots and sat in his room all afternoon pretending to be going down the slopes. When the noises stopped it was early May and all the snow had melted.

The school bus came at 7:30. Ray was on the bus and Guy sat next to him not knowing what to say. Guy thought Ray would be crying. But Ray did not cry. Guy spent the whole day staring at Ray's eyes waiting for the tears to start rolling down his friend's cheek. Their teacher was acting weird. She did not give them homework.

"I want you to write a poem," she told the class. "School will be ending early for summer vacation because of the problems and we'll spend the last day of school around the pool in our swimsuits."

Guy whispered something in Ray's ear about the teacher in a swimsuit. Ray laughed out loud. He laughed and laughed. Guy wondered if he would ever laugh if his mother died.

When Guy got home that evening, his grandfather was there. His mother was still at work.

"I have to write a poem Grandpa," Guy said, hugging his grandfather.

"Yes, but first we have to eat," his grandfather told him.

"You got pizza with olives?" Guy said. Snoopy started jumping all over him. Guy pushed him away.

As they ate Guy felt something was not right.

"Why is Mom not home yet?"

"She called to say she'll be late. She has a meeting," his grandfather said, giving him another slice of pizza.

Guy could not eat much. He wanted his mother to come home.

Guy and his grandfather watched cartoons. His grandfather had white hair and a white moustache. He lived in the mountains and had four dogs. He watched cartoons every night.

"Why do you like cartoons, Grandpa?"

"I don't know. They're better than watching the news," said his grandfather, cracking another walnut in his palm. "They make me laugh."

His mother came home late that evening. Guy was in bed. He was not asleep and he heard his mother telling her father that her job would be transferring soon. Guy ran into the living room. "What does transferring mean?" he asked.

"It means to go from one country to another," his mother said hugging him.

She was holding a big glass in her hand with ice in it and the strong smelling stuff that only his grandfather drank.

"But I don't want to go. I want to stay here," Guy said. "Your breath smells weird," he told his mother.

"Guy, nothing is definite yet. Please go back to sleep" She took him to bed.

"Sing that song you used to sing for me when I was little," he said to his mother as she covered him up with his yellow sheets. She sang *Que Sera Sera whatever will be will be.* She sat with him until he fell asleep. *The future's not ours to see. Que Sera Sera.*

Guy's mother told him that Snoopy should get married. She said he'll get lonely if he doesn't have a wife. She said she would try and find him one. Guy and Snoopy roller-skated back and forth on the balcony almost everyday. Sometimes there was no school and Guy had to spend the whole day at home. The weather was getting real warm but they couldn't go to the beach.

"It's too risky," his mother said.

Ray called one day to tell Guy that he was going away to another country with his grandparents. Guy's mother started packing things into big boxes. She did not go to work anymore. She drank the smelly stuff every night. She was talking on the phone. Guy waited until she hung up and said, "Mom, I have to write a poem and I can't."

His mother twirled the ice in her glass with her fingers. "Choose something you like to have with you all the time," she said, "like Snoopy. I'm sure you can find many things to say about Snoopy."

"What should I say about him? This is hard."

"Don't whine honey. You can't write a poem unless you have a strong feeling about something."

"How will I know when I'm feeling it?" Guy was getting irritated.

"When you dream of it that means you are feeling it very strongly," she said.

"Then what should I do?"

"Then dream the dream again until you can write about it." His mother looked weird. There was blue under her eyes. She talked to Snoopy. "Snoopy, you want to get married, right? Well, I'm trying to find you a wife."

Guy wanted his mother to stop drinking that stuff. He wanted her to stop talking on the phone. He wanted her to stop listening to the radio. He wanted her to stop talking to Snoopy. He wanted her to stop putting their clothes in big boxes.

It was 7:25. The sun was strong. It was the first week in June. Guy stood on the street corner waiting for the school bus. He was wearing his swimsuit under his shorts and a yellow T-shirt. He had his yellow towel under his arm. It was the last day of school and they were going to swim. He had not written a poem. Guy waited for two hours. He looked right and left. He counted the cars that passed. The sun made his hair warm. He was squinting. He refused to believe that the school bus was not coming on the last day of school. At 11:00 he went up to the apartment and held Snoopy.

"The bus will never come, Snoopy," he whispered into the dog's ear.

In his throat, Guy felt a hard object, like a rock, making his voice sound funny and preventing the tears from rising to his eyes.

That night the noises were very loud. His mother got him out of bed and they went down to the basement and sat next to the water boiler until dawn. There were other people sleeping on the floor. The men played cards and listened to the radio. The next day the noises stopped and Guy was able to play in his room with Snoopy. He slid his toy cars back and forth on Snoopy's back, turning it into a highway. Guy's mother had been on the phone all day long. She had put most of their stuff in the big boxes.

Late that afternoon the doorbell rang. Outside the *Khamsin* was blowing again and the sky was very white. Guy heard a man's voice talking to his mother. Then he heard his mother's footsteps coming toward his room. His mother came in and sat next to him on the yellow rug.

"Guy, I have to talk to you. I think I've found a wife for Snoopy." She did not look into Guy's eyes.

"Snoopy doesn't want a wife, do you Snoops?" Guy said. Snoopy licked Guy's ear.

"Guy, my job is transferring and you'll be going to school in another country." His mother played with Snoopy's ears.

"But I don't want to leave," said Guy.

"It's too dangerous for us to stay here. We'll be evacuated soon and we can't take Snoopy with us. He'll be happy with his wife. He can have children, too."

Guy felt something funny in his stomach. Exactly what he felt when he had heard about Ray's mother. Guy's mother carried Snoopy in her arms.

"Snoopy has to go now. Say goodbye to him. If we could take him with us I promise we would. But we have to leave by boat and dogs aren't allowed."

"No, I don't believe you. You're lying," Guy screamed.

His mother ran out carrying Snoopy. Guy sat clutching his toy cars.

He heard the man's footsteps walking away quickly. He suddenly realised what was happening. He ran out of his room. His mother tried to stop him from going out the front door, but he broke free and ran down the stairs.

He saw a red car starting to move. Snoopy was whimpering in the back seat. He was looking at Guy from the rear window. Snoopy howled.

Then the car turned a corner. Snoopy was gone. Guy stood in the street, bewildered. His mother dragged him up the stairs.

"I'm sorry baby, I'm sorry," she told him. "We'll come back soon and we'll get Snoopy back."

"No we won't. We're never coming back here. I know," Guy screamed.

Guy spent that evening by the window. Whenever a red car passed his heart thumped. Was it Snoopy? No. Only the noises became louder and much closer. He slept on his mother's lap in the basement, comforted by the sound of the water boiler.

The next day his mother helped him pack a small bag.

"I want to take my toy cars," said Guy.

"We can't take anything with us but our clothes, baby," his mother said, "we're only allowed one small bag. I'll buy you new cars as soon as we get to our new home, okay?" They were sitting on the bed in Guy's yellow room. Guy felt like something was crushing him. He would feel this many times when he grew up. The feeling that someone was standing on his head and he was sinking in a sea of yellow mud.

Guy wanted to hide in one of the big boxes with all the familiar objects of his childhood. He never wanted to come out. "You are mean," he told his mother. His voice was hoarse as if he had been crying or screaming. "You won't let me take my cars. And Snoopy never wanted to get married. Ever."

The next day Grandpa came and drove them to the port. There were men with machine guns on the streets and the noises were loud. Guy reached for his pen and pencil and started writing. He did not want to look at the men with machine guns. There was lots of smoke everywhere and the air smelled like chalk. He buried his head in his notebook.

When the ship began to move it was dusk. Guy stood on the deck next to his mother, staring out at the burning city. Snoopy, Ray, his toys, his room; he missed them all. He felt the rock in his throat every time he thought of them. He felt a new kind of pain in his stomach, which made him want to be alone. He went off into a corner by himself and read aloud the poem he was writing.

I want to sleep quietly,
But the bombs fall loudly.
I like the mountains and my skis,
But it is too risky.
I want my Snoops to be with me,
But that cannot be.
I love this place and want to stay here,
But the bombs keep getting nearer.

It was dark. A few stars shone down on the deck where Guy was hiding. He did not hear his mother calling him. He had his eyes closed and was dreaming about the many poems he would write. He was dreaming of the yellow room he would have in his new home. He was dreaming of Snoopy's children. In his dream, he was painting them yellow with his finger-paints. He was dreaming of a sea of yellow mud. The man in the red car, holding a machine gun with one hand and Snoopy in the other, was stepping on Guy's head, drowning him in the sea of yellow mud. He would dream of the sea of yellow mud for a very long time.

Cucumber and Mint

In the land of black smoke, there is no room for self-pity.
No one will rise from the ashes of your dead children.

Haas Mroue, *'A Beirut Ghazal'*

Cucumber and Mint

They fled their country one stormy February day. Early in the morning they dragged their suitcases from their second storey apartment and crouched next to a mound of stinking garbage in the doorway of their pockmarked building. Three pairs of expectant eyes waiting for the drone of an engine, the taxi that would carry them off to a safer land.

The city was very still. There was no movement on the streets, no usual clatter from the apartments of mothers preparing school-lunches for their children while listening to the first news bulletin on the radio. The newspaper man who had panted and squeaked his way up the hill to their side of town every morning on his rusted bike, was nowhere to be seen. There was not even the sweet aroma of aniseed cakes wafting through the narrow streets.

The three crouching figures heard a loud hissing noise right over their heads, followed by an explosion that rattled the hollow buildings. Everyone else was in the safety of a shelter or a corridor in anticipation of more shelling and away from the ever-present snipers. Lana, the youngest, covered her ears with her hands to block out the noises, although she kept her eyes wide open. She sat rocking back and forth on her bulging suitcase, humming to herself, unconsciously pulling at her doll's hair, as she stared at the rats noisily rummaging through the garbage. Hana - eight year old - buried her head in her mother's stomach. She had not spoken in two months.

The two daughters and their mother, Tamina, had spend most of these last eight weeks curled up on the cold concrete floor of the underground basement that reeked of stale urine and dirty feet. For days they had lived on nothing but canned sardines and dry biscuits. Dipping her fingers into the oily can of sardines, Tamina would dream of fresh pita to wrap around the tiny pieces of fish. Her daughters refused to eat, complaining that the fish stank and the dry biscuits scratched their throats. "I hate fish Mama. I hate this smell," Lana would say. Sometimes, the neighbour's boy, Bilal would risk the snipers and the shelling and run out to the underground bakery. If there had been enough fuel that day to run the generator to power the electric ovens he would return with a few warm pitas and hand one timidly to Tamina. "Here, Mrs Mutal, I brought you some bread," Bilal would say, lowering his eyes. He never looked into Tamina's eyes. She wondered if the teenager fantasized about seeing her naked, for she was still young and firm. Tamina immediately dismissed the thought from her mind. But most of the time Bilal would return empty handed because there had been no wheat to make bread.

Sometimes the rockets would fall all around their building, about two rockets a minute for twelve hours or more. Lana and Hana would bury their heads in Tamina's lap. And as the three of them lay trembling from the fear and the cold, Tamina could not help but wish for a rocket to somehow find its way into the shelter and kill them all. Instantly. Why had their lives become so primitive? Who was killing who anyway? And for what? She did not want her children to grow up in a country that had no respect for itself or its people. And Tamina did not want her daughters to grow up as immigrants in some foreign land where they would always remain second-class citizens with funny accents.

The girls never complained, and their submissiveness pushed Tamina to take some action. She could not bear to see her daughters' skin so yellow, their eyes so slow to react to any movement and their limbs so weak and tender. They needed milk and she had to go up to the apartment and get some. But the snipers were there, on the rooftops of the surrounding buildings waiting for any movement. They had even shot at the two cats that were always prowling around the corridors. Bilal found them lying in a pool of blood on his balcony.

Tamina removed her shawl and sweater and placed them under the heads of her two sleeping daughters and slowly crawled on her hands and feet up the sixty-eight steps that led to her apartment. She could not walk upright as the snipers would spot her immediately. There was no glass on the windows; it had all shattered the first day of the shelling, and the glass lay in tiny pieces, carpeting the floor. As Tamina crawled towards her apartment, she did not feel the pieces of glass entering her palms, did not see the blood oozing out. Not until she had reached for the half empty can of powdered milk and crawled back down to the basement with bullets racing over her head, did she notice the blood pouring out of her hands. But Bilal had already run up to her with an old T-shirt that he had split in half and helped her wrap the cloth around each hand until the bleeding stopped.

"Does it hurt much?" he asked timidly.

"No, Bilal. I'm fine. Thanks."

He then trampled over a few sleeping bodies in his rush to return to his side of the basement where his family lay huddled, staring at Tamina as if she had gone mad.

Peering down into the large can of milk, Tamina realised that she had no water to mix the powder with. She hugged her two girls and held them close to her chest and whispered, "You will remember this day because you will not drink the milk but eat it." She gave each girl a spoonful of the white powder and watched, smiling, as it dissolved in their mouths, sticking to their tongues. Tamina could not stop the civil war but she was going to make sure her daughters were well nourished and healthy. They had to be ready for the long trip to America to join their father. He had taken all their savings and was going to buy a small grocery store. He had promised to send for them as soon as he could get their residency papers approved. That had been nine months ago. Tamina prayed every night that the next day she would receive a letter from her husband with the airline tickets and visas and the family could be reunited and start a new life.

The rain had turned into a light drizzle falling over the smouldering city as the taxi pulled up in front of the three squatting figures. The driver, an elderly man, was bald and had little black eyes that darted back and forth, not focusing on anything. "Please hurry before the snipers see us," he said, rushing to open the trunk. As he lifted the suitcases into the old Mercedes, Tamina wondered if she would ever be able to extinguish the fire that slowly began to rage in her heart. Even Lana stopped humming as they pulled away, the tires screeching. Tamina's eyes were glued to the building that she had lived in for eleven years of her life. They turned a corner and Tamina could only see the rain sliding down the windshield.

Lana's eyes were wide open, her nose pressed up against the dirty window of the taxi, as they began climbing up the mountain road that would eventually wind down and lead them to the border, then Damascus. It had stopped raining and the sky was partly blue, partly dark grey. As they gained altitude the earth smelled sweet, as it had smelled after the spring rains in Tamina's village. Tamina looked back for the first time at the city they were fleeing, and to the sea beyond it. How serene the blue water seemed. A pine tree forest was burning in the distance. Tamina could not bear to watch the smoke rising; already half the city was covered with a thick black cloud. She looked straight ahead and resumed the unconscious tugging of her shawl, a nervous habit she had picked up during the shelter days. Her shawl was slowly being shredded to tiny pieces. Tamina had the overwhelming desire to return to her village, a little girl, to climb up the old fig tree and hide in its shade and look out toward the sea. "It's not fair, it's just not fair," she thought to herself. When her brother took her doll away and buried it in the mud she cried in her tree for hours, mumbling "It's not fair," out loud. Her throat ached, her temples throbbed. Her mother finally convinced little Tamina to come down from the tree and hugged her and helped her wash the mud off the doll. Maybe if she cried now, Raad would come and hold her. Together they would go back home and sweep the glass off the floor. Then maybe he would make love to her on the Oriental rug in the living room and hold her in his arms for a long, long time.

A powerful explosion shook the ground they drove on and she awoke from her trance as Hana pressed her head deeper into her lap. Lana continued to watch intently all that they were passing - the vegetable vendors selling eggplants and squash behind stands surrounded with sandbags to protect them from the shrapnel, the piles and piles of uncollected garbage, and the many cars loaded with belongings heading away from the city. One car had a huge mattress strapped flat to the roof. "Mama, look, look at the moving bed," cried Lana.

But Tamina was too tired to look, too engrossed in her thoughts, her mixed emotions about leaving. She had felt so secure the night before in the shelter, it had become her second home. There had been a short-lived cease-fire and she was able to go to her apartment and pack a few suitcases. Now that she was heading for the unknown, she longed for the familiarity of the cold concrete floors. She had received a letter from Raad the day before, along with the airline tickets. He had sent them with an official from the army who arranged for this taxi to take them to Damascus airport. Raad had given all their savings to a Mexican man who would smuggle them across the border into San Diego where Raad would be waiting for them. To be poor and together in America is better than living with bombs and snipers in our country, Raad had written in his letter. A farm in Fresno had promised him a job picking cherries in June. Tamina did not want to think what life would be like. Her husband a laborer? They had owned a Falafel shop down in the old *souk*. Then the war came and their shop became part of the green line that divided the city. Raad had not lived with them since Lana was a toddler. First he went to Kuwait, then Saudi Arabia. And now America. But this time he seemed determined to make a new life. 'They have public schools here,' he had written, 'our daughters will get a good education. And there is a swimming pool nearby where the girls can swim in the summer. The television programmes are on all day, you will not be lonely,' Raad had written.

Tamina did miss her husband tremendously. But she had had second thoughts about leaving. If she left she knew she would never return. Her apartment would surely be looted and destroyed. And what is this new life that Raad talked about? How long could they remain illegal without being caught? What if they were deported? They had no home to go back to. And why did they have to fly to Mexico City and then take a bus for hours and then walk across a river at night? They don't give visas to people from war-torn countries, Raad had told her. What about all those films she had seen about the big ships arriving at Ellis Island during the big wars filled with Europeans destined to make a new life for themselves and their families. Why were they different? Why couldn't she legally make a new life for herself and her family? Tamina tried hard not to think. Her mind was bursting with thoughts. So many things could happen. In less than an hour she would become an immigrant. A stranger in every land she would go to. A refugee. How she hated that word 'refugee'. It reminded her of tents and flies and open sewers.

They stopped in *Chtaura* for breakfast - thin layers of *markouk* bread filled with *kechkaval* cheese, cucumber and fresh mint. Their first real meal in days. The driver insisted on paying and Tamina thanked him endlessly. "God bless your children", she told him over and over again, "thank you, thank you." Tamina and the girls stood outside looking down towards the valley and the city from which they had just come. The sun had emerged strong after the storm and it was getting real warm even at such a high altitude. Tamina and Lana took their sweaters off. "Hana, aren't you warm in that wool sweater?" Tamina asked. Hana shook her head. On warm, clear days like today Tamina would usually take her girls to the beach to play on the sand. The almond trees would soon bloom in this very valley where Tamina stood; like little specks of soft white clouds the almond blossoms would fill the valley. But Tamina would not be here. She turned around and faced the snow-capped mountains in the distance. Why couldn't she live up there, she asked herself, on top of the mountain? I want to go home, Tamina thought, realising that the word 'home' would have no meaning as soon as she crossed the border. She could still turn back. What if she told the driver that she wanted to go back to Beirut, to walk along the beach? Then she remembered the snipers and the rockets and Raad waiting for them. They climbed back into the car and the driver, his mouth full of food, explained to Tamina that it would be real warm in Damascus today.

The girls had already devoured their sandwiches and fell asleep as soon as the car started moving. Tamina swallowed the last bite of hers, rolled down her window, and breathed deeply from the mountain air of her country. They were nearing the border control and Tamina closed her eyes wanting to picture what she was heading for. Life in America. She would become an extension of Raad, dependent on him for everything. She would cook for him everyday. She would be happy the first few days. But after washing away the smell of sardines from her clothes and knitting herself a new shawl, she would again feel the fire in her heart. She wondered how long it would be before her heart turned to ashes.

Tamina's breathing had become very slow as she slipped into a form of restful meditation and she began to see images in colour. She saw Lana's orange swimming trunks floating in a swimming pool, her daughter's face all blue and swollen. She saw Raad sitting in a pool of blood on a white sofa, the TV flickering purple shadows across his limp body in the darkness. Tamina heard a scream. She gasped for air and opened her eyes. They were in line for the final border checkpoint and an elderly woman was screaming at the customs officer who was confiscating her container of little *ma'amoul* cakes. "Please son," she was saying, "I spent all my money on the butter and the sugar, may God protect your children, let me through with the sweets. Have pity on an old woman like me."

Tamina's breathing was erratic; she was trying hard not to sob. She closed her eyes again, desperately clinging to her country, walking through her apartment in her mind, not wanting to forget years later and regret not having paid attention to even the slightest detail. The car began to move and Tamina knew that they had crossed the border. She remained, eyes closed, sitting very still, trying to reverse time. She suddenly saw herself back in her kitchen, hands scratched and bloody, crawling on the floor. She wished that she had stood up then and leaned out the open window and faced the sniper. She wished the sniper had aimed right at her forehead and blown her head off. She wished her brains had splattered all over the kitchen walls. She wished her brains were anywhere but here, registering the fact that her daughters would grow up as refugees with delirious memories of a childhood scarred with violence and hostility.

"Welcome to Damascus," the driver was telling her.

"What? We're there?" asked Tamina in a weak voice

"Almost. Five more miles."

Tamina opened her eyes and the glare of the sun against the black asphalt almost blinded her. She was now officially a refugee. Glancing at her two daughters sleeping next to her, she realized that they possessed nothing of their country except the cucumber and mint leaves that were being broken down in their stomachs. "Please, would you stop for a minute," Tamina asked the driver, her voice calm, controlled.

The driver stopped at the side of the road. Tamina opened her door slightly, stuck her head out and emptied her insides on the warm, loose gravel just outside Damascus.

Civil War

On a balcony of a bombed-out skyscraper
I dangle my soul out for you.
Snipers, where are you?
Don't ignore me now.

Haas Mroue, *'Civil War'*

Civil War

You don't think of dying as you walk the streets alone, an AK-47 slung over your shoulder. A starry January night and the streets are deserted. It is cold and you have a joint in your pocket. You hear sounds of machine gun fire from the Green Line, that imposed divide that splits east from west. It is followed by the hiss of Howitzers. An RPG then fires in reply. The front is six blocks away but here you feel safe patrolling the streets of the Hotel District. Your militia drove the enemy out in December and now you pass the St. George Hotel, which you helped liberate during the War of the Hotels.

You stand by the deserted St. George pool and remember the time when you were ten and you and your friends would climb the whitewashed walls surrounding it and stare at the blonde women in bikinis. You watched them as they swam on their backs and you wondered if you would ever hold a blonde woman's wet body to your chest. You watched them as they sipped drinks from tall glasses with tiny umbrellas and orange wedges stuck to the glass. You had never seen such small umbrellas and you wish you could have had one to stick in your teacup at home. But you were chased away by the hotel guards shouting obscenities at you and your friends. "Go back to the camps where you belong," they would scream as you ran up the hill, inland.

Now you look at the wall. The moon shines down on it, bullet holes riddle it. You have the pool to yourself. A pool filled with black water and wet leaves. You take a few steps closer to the sea, to what was once the bar terrace. You hear the Mediterranean lapping against concrete. In the distance, red lines streak across the sky and disappear and then the ground shudders slightly. You see a red shirt floating in the water. It does not surprise you. All the militias dump their corpses into the sea. You and your friends control this area now and you hope the body floating in the water is not someone you knew.

You turn around and look inland at the deserted apartment buildings facing the sea. People lived here just six months ago. Mothers cooked meals and families would sip coffee on balconies overlooking the sea. Children waited for the schoolbus at corners.

You walk slowly up the hill. You hear the soft voice of an opera singer drifting from the Holiday Inn. It is close to midnight and the noises from the front are getting more consistent. You walk into the lobby where the music gets louder.

Bjorg must be working, you think. You walk up the sixteen flights of steps. The red velvet carpet beneath your feet has turned black since your last visit. It reeks of smoke from the rocket that crashed here a few days before. You call out to Bjorg but the music drowns your voice.

On the sixteenth floor Bjorg sits by an open window, his rifle aimed Eastward, his ghetto blaster next to him. You don't know much about opera, but the woman's voice is deep, warm.

Bjorg, the sniper from Holland, shakes your hand. He knew you were coming, he saw you in the viewfinder of his rifle. You sit next to him. The breeze from the window caresses your hair. Bjorg gives you his joint. You feel good. You do not have to think of other days. You take a hit. Bjorg sees something in his viewfinder and fires. You wish you could be like him. You pass him the joint and raise your eyebrows. He switches the tape recorder off.

"Oh, just a cat," he says, dragging deep on the joint.

You can see he hasn't shaved in a week. He is thin. His face is all eyes. The color of his skin is a deep yellow, like the color of apricots in summer.

"What's the count today?" You ask.

Bjorg takes a swig from the bottle of Red Label.

"Three men in army fatigues and two civilians in a red VW," Bjorg says rubbing his yellow teeth with his fingers. "And the cat."

You take a long drink from the bottle of whisky. Your head starts to spin and you remember that you have not eaten since breakfast. You wish Bjorg would teach you how to kill. Maybe if you kill enough you will stop being afraid. You lay your head down on the remains of the red carpet and close your eyes.

You wake up when the ceasefire takes hold at dawn. Bjorg gets ready to sleep. You give him the joint from your pocket and tell him you'll be back to visit again soon.

You leave the Holiday Inn with your AK-47 as the sun is emerging from behind the snow-capped Mount Sannine. You walk Westward, away from the sun. You don't look East at the bridge. You don't want to see a VW with two dead people in it. You pass the French Embassy and stop to smoke a Gitane with the French marine who guards the entrance. He stands behind slabs of concrete and barbed wire. You pass by here often and he knows you. You talk using sign language and the few French words you learned at school. You ask him about Paris and he tells you about the girls in a place called St. Denis. He makes groaning noises and laughs.

"Someday I'll go to Paris," you say and walk on.

Mornings are ceasefire time; an unwritten rule. The streets are no longer yours. Vegetable vendors push their carts, stopping in the shade of an old fig tree to sell their produce to elderly couples with newspapers under their arms. The women pull closer to their husbands when they see you and your machine gun. The men nod and quickly lower their eyes to the pavement.

You stop at the bakery. There is a long queue, but people make way for you. You buy a meat pie and munch on it as you walk. You pass the American University and notice two girls in tight skirts carrying notebooks. The smell of soap and perfume arouses you. You smell your underarms and decide to go home.

In the service taxi the radio is on. The names of yesterday's casualties are being read. Claude and Mona in a red VW are reported missing. You light a cigarette. You wonder if Claude and Mona were lovers. You hope they died instantly. You thank the driver and give him your Marlboros. He doesn't expect you to pay him. You are in the neighborhood where you grew up and the streets are full of shoppers and vendors and children running around pulling at your sleeve, wanting to play war with you. They shoot you with imaginary machine guns.

"Go to school," you shout at them.

"There is no school," they chant.

You haven't been home for five days and you forget there are people living relatively normal lives. You walk through alleyways filled with puddles and spent bullets. You pause for a minute in front of your apartment building. The yellow paint is peeling. The walls are riddled with bullet holes and shrapnel.

You jump over the wall and onto the balcony of the ground floor apartment. Your mother is frying onions in the kitchen. You want to cry at the smell. You want to hug your mother. You want to bury your head in her bosom and take in the smell of fried onions, Clorox and lavender. But instead you ask, "What's for breakfast?"

You catch her by surprise. She has the radio on and did not hear you come in. She takes your hands in hers and looks into eyes.

"You've been drinking again," she says. She turns away and stirs the onions in the old pan.

You think that when the war is over you will buy her a new pan - one of those Teflon ones you saw on a commercial on TV with that blonde woman making eggs that never stick.

Your mother in her black dress puts a big pot of water on the burner for your bath. You go to your room and take off your clothes. She comes in after you, silently collecting your jacket and pants and underwear. You cover yourself with your hands. You don't want her to see you naked. She brings the pot of steaming water and puts it in the bathroom for you. You want to say something, say thank you. You want to tell her that you love her. You want to tell her that you haven't killed anybody.

After you bathe you eat in the kitchen. She fries you eggs and cheese. She slices tomatoes and cucumber. She puts olives in a little dish.

"I made these from your uncle's tree," she says.

You nod, your mouth full. You wish you hadn't given your last joint to Bjorg. You watch your mother moving around in her small kitchen. Her black dress is stained with white flour and olive oil. The radio she listens to is covered with dirt. You want to buy her a new radio. You want to take her away from this kitchen, somewhere where she can have her own olive tree, away from this city and its smoke and shrapnel and flooded streets.

You sleep until evening. By nightfall the rockets from the Green Line are too strong to ignore. The power is out. Your mother sits in the living room by candlelight knitting a sweater. You wonder if it is for you. She hears you getting up, going to the bathroom, and she goes to the kitchen to get your coffee. You sit facing her in the dark living room and listen to the rockets. You sip your coffee quickly. She smiles at you. She wants you to talk to her. You feel restless. You want to be outside, on the streets. You want to hold your AK-47. You want to feel the wind in your hair. She doesn't even look up when you go to your bedroom and walk out carrying your machine gun.

"May God be with you," she says under her breath as you walk out the front door.

There's a curfew and the streets are deserted again. The cool wind against your face makes you feel strong again. You walk quickly, taking long steps. You walk the two miles down to the sea and walk along the Corniche towards the Hotel District. You decide to stop at headquarters on your way. The old house with a red tiled roof was a famous restaurant before the militia took over. The guys lounge around, smoking. They greet you warmly. They all know a sniper bullet might get you any time around the hotels and you see the look of pity in their eyes. You couldn't kill and they all know it. You try not to think of that first battle when you were manning the Dushka mounted on a pick-up truck. A family on the enemy side had refused to leave their apartment in an area that your militia had captured. You were supposed to fire a rocket into their home but instead you aimed at the deserted apartment above. The family was only slightly injured. The militia gave you the option of quitting or becoming a guard, patrolling the street alone.

They did not even give you grenades, just a machine gun.

Tonight they all pump your hand and thump you on the shoulder as if you were a hero. "How is our hotel man," they all say.

Everyone is a hypocrite, you think. Even people who kill.

Most of the men sit on the terrace, under the pine trees. Whisky bottles and cigarette butts litter the ground. The news from the front is good. Only two killed from your side tonight. You walk around, listening to the wind playing with the pine trees. You don't stop to talk to anyone. You grab a bottle of Red Label from the crate in the hallway and walk out.

You see a jeep screeching towards you. A few soldiers are standing, holding on to the windshield. As the jeep passes you, you see a man's body tied to the back of the vehicle. The body makes a noise like a broom against asphalt. The corpse is sweeping your streets. The corpse is probably a man your age, you think, eighteen or nineteen or twenty. You wonder what his mother is doing on the East side of town now. You wonder if she will cook breakfast in the morning.

The wind is strong tonight. There are no stars. It smells like rain. As you walk towards the hotels a bullet whizzes past your head. You jump on the rocks and walk closer to the water. The waves hit your boots and your feet get wet. The noise of the battle is diminished here. All you hear is the waves. And the wind. You climb up the wall onto the terrace of the St. George Hotel. You sit facing the sea.

It starts to rain and the wind makes the rain fly. You look towards the East and wonder what is East and what is West. And with the wind in your hair and the rain in your eyes you pray for Claude and Mona and your father and the corpse behind the jeep and the cat that Bjorg killed. You pray for your country, for your city divided in two.

You are sitting on the terrace of the St. George Hotel Bar but you are falling.

Beirut is falling.

Everyone is falling.

You know that if a man drags another man like a child drags his toy duck then someone is falling. And you just want the wind in your hair. You just want the rain in your eyes, on your lips, trickling down your back.

You wonder if the men in the jeep, who could have been your classmates in high school, you wonder if they cut up the man behind their jeep. You wonder if they cut off his parts and put them in a plastic bag and threw them to the fish in the sea. You wonder if your children will eat fish that fed on human flesh, your neighbor's flesh, your classmates' flesh.

You want to start over. You want to forget the day last April when your friends called you up and asked you to demonstrate with them. You want to forget the day the militia distributed machine guns to everyone in the neighbourhood. And you, bored of sitting at home with no job and no money, signed up. "I'm becoming a fighter," you told your mother.

You want to forget the months spent training in the camps. They applauded your precision. "He has an eye," they all said.

It was still a game. The battles hadn't started yet. Then you were manning a checkpoint downtown near Martyrs Square. A man in a Renault 5 did not stop. You fired. His wife or his sister or his mother - you don't remember - got out and screamed for help. The man could still walk. The bullet settled in his neck and his shirt was wet with blood. You let him fall in the mud and pointed the gun at the woman who started running away.

You sit facing the sea and think of that woman. You hope she left this city forever. You hope she will never come back. You hope she retrieved the man's body and buried him in a grave. You hope she put flowers on the grave before she went away. But you know wherever that woman is she will be falling.

You know she will forever remember your face.

She sees your face at night as she tries to sleep. The face of the man with the machine gun. You wish you could go away and look for this woman. You want to show her your eyes. You remember that she was frail and thin. You want to put your arms around her. You want to spend the rest of your life with her.

But with the wind in your hair you know you will always be here and you will kill again someday. You will fall with your city. You will kill before your enemy takes over your area and kills your mother. You will have to drink and smoke and joke with the guys. You will have to cheer them on when they drag a corpse behind their jeep. You will have to live with your own sweat for days and not think that the enemy a mile down the road might be someone you went to school with, maybe he had been a friend. But he will fight for the East and you will fight for the West.

And the newspapers call this a civil war.

The wind is strong and it plays with your hair. You take off your jacket and shirt. You take off your white undershirt and wave it to the wind, just as you had seen the Indians doing in cowboy movies. You want to walk East with the white shirt flapping in the wind. But you stay sitting, staring at the blackness of the horizon and think of your grandmother. You would sit on her terrace, under the grapevine, and stare out at the sea.

"What's after the horizon, Grandma?" you remember asking her.

"After the horizon, *ya albi*, is where all the dead people are," she tells

32

you and she would peel figs and oranges and pomegranates on her terrace for you.

"But Grandma, there must be something else out there," you remember saying.

"No, *ya habibi*, there's only dead people."

Beyond the Horizon

'We are all refugees. We drift through places like pollen in
May. We don't water our roots. We take warm baths and
remember washing with a Sohat bottle during those days
of war.'

Haas Mroue, 'Days of War'

Beyond the Horizon

I'm flying at 33,000 feet somewhere over Pennsylvania and I think of Amoulaki. How I miss Amoulaki. I feel anger when I think of her. I did nothing to help her stay.

As I look down from the airplane window at the green countryside, I remember the good times we had last summer. The long drives, the laughter, the love. Days where nothing happened, days that I could easily forget but yet I remember vividly because I was with Amoulaki. She whose needs were so few and who was forced to go back to a country that smothers even the humblest of dreams. I pray that Amoulaki is not slipping into chronic depression, I hope she will not cease searching for a way to flee the land that once promised so much love and showed such warmth; the land that deceived us all.

Amoulaki's freshly washed hair smells of apples. Taking a warm bath is Amoulaki's most effective way to distance herself from her sadness. But the water is cold during these days of war. The whiskey glass – no ice – rests on the bookshelf next to Amoulaki's bed where she sits gently brushing her wet hair. She takes a gulp and waits for the liquid to turn to fire and warm her insides. Another gulp and now Amoulaki lays her head on the pillow and dreams of an underwater world where dolphins carry machine guns and shoot at passing schools of fish. A fish asks a dolphin, "Why won't you leave us in peace?"

"Because if we don't kill you the octopuses will," the dolphin answers. "But if you join us and help us kill the octopuses we will stop shooting you."

The fish being weak, and having no means of self-defense, ally themselves with the dolphins, working with them to eliminate all octopuses from the waters. But the dolphins soon get bored of ambushing octopuses. The octopuses sense the dolphins' weariness and offer them an alliance instead. The dolphins accept and join forces with the octopuses to start to slaughter all the fish again. Amoulaki wakes up breathing heavily, her temples throbbing, a foul taste in her mouth. An octopus has been clinging to her neck, his eight arms drowning her in a sea of red mud. And outside, between the swaying fern trees, the shells have not stopped falling.

Amoulaki walks slowly on the narrow mountain road, delicately treading the earth, the same earth that covers her grandfather's bones in the nearby cemetery. She collects what is left of the spring flowers, her hair still damp, her breath smelling of wild roses and tobacco. Amoulaki hums quietly, a hum of a prisoner who has succeeded in repressing the fierce desire to escape. Amoulaki waits for her saviour. She patiently waits for the moment to exult at the sight of her homeland dissolving with the dust in the distance. The cool breeze caresses her hair as I stop my car next to her. She looks up but doesn't smile.

"Forgive me Amoulaki, I'm late, l had to wait for a lull in the fighting."

She gets in next to me and without touching me she lays the flowers on my lap. We go fast. Very fast. The car leaves the ground and starts to fly, it has turned into an airplane. We fly over the Hotel, Amoulaki's home, but she doesn't look back, she looks West, towards the setting sun, knowing I'll take her to civilization. We fly faster than the speed of sound, Amoulaki and I, away from this hell to a new land. It may not be a perfect land, and possibly far from civilized, but it is a place where the mind and the body can be free.

Goodbye cowards, goodbye murderers. May God help you be free from the oppression you have brought unto yourselves. Goodbye what was once paradise. May your dead children's blood fertilize the land and may you reap something other than corpses during the next harvest.

We are still flying fast. I look over at Amoulaki, wanting to break the silence. But she is gone. The flowers have wilted on my lap.

I wake up sweating. Where is Amoulaki?

She is still picking flowers on the Road of the Lovers. Watch out Amoulaki! Watch out for the shells, the rockets, the bombs. Beware. Run to the shelter. Run! Inhale those sweet fumes, the pride of the *Bekaa* valley. They will help you escape. They will get you closer to me. They will enable you to remember better days.

Days like those Amoulaki spent in the village at her grandmother's house when she was just a child.

Amoulaki sits next to her grandma on the terrace under the ripening grapes, as they both gaze out at the endless ocean.

"What is there after the sea, Grandma?" Amoulaki asks.

"The horizon," grandma answers.

"What's that?"

"It's the line that you see way out there, where the sky joins the sea."

"What can you see from there?"

"Nothing."

"But grandma, what's after the horizon?"

"Nothing, little one, nothing."

"So when we die do we go there?"

"Why do you say that?"

"Because when we die we become nothing, don't we?"

"Yes," grandma whispers.

Amoulaki sees herself sitting on the horizon, her legs dangling, her back to the world, as she looks beyond the horizon at all the dead people. Her daydreams are interrupted by a few of grandma's old lady friends who have come to visit. They sit and gossip as they sip their orange blossom lemonades. How Amoulaki loves to watch them. She loves going down to the dark basement where earlier she had helped her grandmother press the olives into oil. She would then emerge loaded with bars of olive soap and hand them out to the guests. "Grandma and I made them," she would say proudly.

But the village was invaded, the house destroyed, the olive trees razed and the grapes crushed. And grandma became a refugee. Amoulaki's world shrank and she was doomed to remain in the war-torn city, living among those with complicated attitudes, bourgeois desires and superhuman needs. Amoulaki finds herself surrounded by people who love only if they are given something in return.

Amoulaki deserves a world full of unselfish love, a place where money and murders are as alien as dinosaurs. And I wish I could give that world to Amoulaki. I would live in a clay hut on top of a mountain and build Amoulaki another hut at the top of the facing mountain. From my hut I would survey the whole land and guard it from any potential invaders, from anyone who might harm Amoulaki. Every Sunday we would meet under the fig tree that lay halfway between my mountain and hers and we would have lunch. We would eat olives, wild thyme and pomegranates. Amoulaki would wave to the shepherd and his goats. For once, she would not be aching to be somewhere away from this land, but would be content with where she was. She'd love the clouds just as clouds, not as a means of escape, and as every star appeared Amoulaki would be there to greet it.

But early in the morning we would not wake up. The fighter jets would have come in the night and dropped their load of bombs on our mountains. Our huts would have exploded into millions of tiny bits of clay.

At 33,000 feet, over Kansas now, and still thinking of Amoulaki.

I was with Amoulaki in October on that plane that took her home.

Home?

I was with Amoulaki on that plane that took her from JFK to the place she loathed most. I sat quietly somewhere deep within her and watched her heart heaving as the plane landed. It was as if someone had wrapped Amoulaki's heart with a black veil and then tied a big rock to that veil. Coming back to a war torn country somewhere in the third world. Home. A place where brother kills brother for the sake of power. And religion.

That cursed thing they call religion, pulling everyone apart, maiming, blinding, massacring…

As Amoulaki walked down the steps from the plane she took a deep breath of the humid air smelling of fish and aircraft fuel. When her feet touched the ground all her muscles relaxed. "My country," she whispered under her breath. But when she looked up she saw those ugly bearded men cradling their machine guns, and every muscle in her fragile body began to ache again. There was a driver there to meet her, waiting nervously among the crowd of people behind the railings – too dangerous for her family to come to the airport. Amoulaki could not talk much as they drove away. She wanted to be left alone. Alone with her memories. But the car was moving down a crowded road and she could not help noticing the many men brandishing machine guns. And the women idolizing them, encouraging them, some from behind a veil, with a slight movement of their eyes. Amoulaki felt like screaming at the driver to stop the car, getting out, running through the streets and shouting, "What are you fighting for? All this for what?" She wanted to take their guns away and then hug them all, embrace them and hold them close, all those people that walked on the street, those people that were born on the same land as she. But from somewhere there was shooting and the people scrambled to take cover as the driver accelerated and Amoulaki closed her eyes repressing the hate she felt. Who gives them the guns?

At one of the roadblocks that abound in the city, a young teenage boy, his face covered with acne, demanded to see Amoulaki's passport. In the car ahead, Amoulaki could see an elderly couple being harassed by another teenager, his machine gun slung nonchalantly over his shoulder. Both the old man and woman had their heads bowed, their eyes to the ground, while the boy checked their identity cards. They had bowed their heads all their lives in their own country. A country full of cowards, submissive oppressed cowards. Amoulaki looked straight into the boy's eyes, large ignorant eyes, as he flipped the pages of her passport. Eyes that could almost be innocent, but they had been taught to see only the bad, the ugly, and to blink only at the sight of their revered leader, some vile human being who stole the boy's childhood and brainwashed this tiny mind.

"You were in America?" he asks, his voice almost a man's but not quite. Amoulaki does not lower her eyes.

"Yes," she says.

The boy sighs deeply then waves his machine gun, signalling for the driver to move on. Many days later Amoulaki would see this boy's face in a dream, a happy laughing face but with no eyes, just two big gaping holes. As the car lurches forward, Amoulaki looks back and sees the boy still staring at her. She smiles. Yes, she had been in America, at peace with herself at last. But she had been an alien. An illegal alien deported back to this hell, while the world cried over two lost whales somewhere near the North Pole. She had always thought that aliens were disgusting slimy creatures that fed on human flesh, creatures that were gunned down by handsome Hollywood actors. Amoulaki could not help feeling pity, not only for the boy, the elderly couple and all the other people, but for herself, too.

When Amoulaki saw the sea she relaxed. Why was she making a big deal about coming back? It's a beautiful land. But beautiful lands, like good people, are cursed. Good people die young. Beautiful lands are burned.

After Amoulaki arrived home, her cheeks still warm from her parent's kisses, despair began setting in. The longing for a faraway land returned. Her parents were blind. They never knew of the black veil that enveloped Amoulaki's heart, nor could they see the blue circles that were appearing under her large brown eyes. And Amoulaki knew that when Spring came the flowers would not bloom.

But Amoulaki manages to go on. She still drives down to work every day in the records department at the hospital, sitting in that smoke–filled room that reeks with the smell of Turkish coffee and old forgotten files. Files of the many wounded, the mental wounds of almost two decades of war. By late afternoon Amoulaki longs to fly far from all that surrounds her, longs to run away from these records of atrocities that suffocate her with their barbarity. But Amoulaki knows that even if she does succeed in leaving, her nights, wherever she may be, will be filled with violent dreams to carry her to her dying day.

Why can't your car have wings, Amoulaki? Then one day after work, while speeding down the highway, you can take off into the blue sky, roll down your window and feel the cool wind against your face. Then let your hair fly as you steer our way. Don't forget your sunglasses, Amoulaki; the sun is strong at 33,000 feet.

From my little window I see a car. A little blue Fiat flying alongside the huge aircraft, and Amoulaki is waving to me. "Come fly with me," she calls.

"I'm coming Amoulaki, wait for me. I can't open this window Wait. Amoul. Wait!"

The blue Fiat is racing through the streets. The sea is calm, a few white clouds float past ever so peacefully. Amoulaki is driving fast, heading towards the mountains, away from the sea. A loud explosion. And another. A shell crashes on the road in front of the Fiat. A few splinters fall on the hood of the car as it swerves out of control. Your car doesn't have wings, Amoulaki. Get on that cloud, it'll take you away from this madness. Climb up on that cloud and you will see everything from up there. You will see the people huddled in their shelters, the children whimpering from fear. You will see the soldiers loading their weapons under the hot summer sun, hatred burning in their eyes. You will see the politicians rubbing their hands in glee, calling a superpower for more weapons, while the dismembered remains of their citizens fill the hospital freezers. And from up there, on your little cloud, you will smell the evaporating blood mixed with the burning pine trees and gunpowder. And you will vomit. Vomit until it covers all the land. Vomit the fear, the oppression, the whiskey, and your lost loves. You will cleanse your system of the hatred within. Hatred that is not directed at anyone or anything in particular, except maybe yourself.

The white cloud is now heading towards the ocean, towards the horizon. Goodbye insanity. Goodbye. From my little window at 33, 000 feet I see a cloud and on it sits Amoulaki, her legs dangling over the side, smoking a cigarette. I long to touch her to make sure she is safe and warm. She smiles. Her beautiful teeth are still intact. Dark clouds form overhead. Thunder. The wind is pushing Amoulaki's cloud away. A flash of lightning. The airplane shudders. Amoulaki has disappeared. I am left alone, slumped in my seat, shivering, heading towards Los Angeles.

Amoulaki cries, trembling violently.
Amoulaki laughs hysterically.
Amoulaki, you are like your country. You don't know whether to laugh at the stupidity of the whole thing, or weep at the helplessness that you're drowning in.

Amoulaki, where are you,? Hold on, don't let go. I wish I could promise you that it will be over soon. What has begun will never end: A third world country at war with itself.

A third world country that thought itself civilized. A country that welcomed invaders with a shower of rice, then stabbed them in the back with a dull knife.

No more children will be born in your homeland, Amoulaki. The women's wombs have become graves, for the women no longer bear children but shrivelled clumps of blood that will never breathe. The men will never marry, they no longer know love, for they feed on the rotting flesh that litters their streets.

And the young think of nothing but revenge, the constant on-going hunger for revenge. It is this longing that will finally annihilate your people from the face of this earth. Those who tell you it will end soon are desperate creatures that have lost their soul. But who am I to judge? Amoulaki, I can only tell you what I see.

I see a country where hatred runs instead of blood in the arteries of its people. And I see a land abused. A land can only take so much. Soon there will be no more fresh water to quench the thirst of your people. For in the deep crevices of the earth the water is turning into a thick liquid, and from the springs you will soon drink the warm pus that gushes out from the infected soil. And the music that once flowed through the canyons and echoed in the valleys has been replaced with the bitter silence of regret.

And no one will mourn. It's too late even for that. All you can do is look for that peaceful mountain, wherever it may be, be it thousands of miles away from your land, and make it your home. You won't be a deserter, for every single one of us is a deserter, a traitor in our own way.

But you will never read these words I now write. For the imbeciles that have descended from the desert to claim our lush lands will confiscate this letter at the border.

Amoulaki. Amoulaki. I want to say your name over and over, maybe you will hear me. What would I tell you if you could hear? That I love you and will be waiting for you. I will be there waiting for the cloud with you on it.

The plane has landed. In an hour, I will be home. Home on a mountain overlooking Los Angeles.

And I will sit and watch the clouds and gaze at the horizon, keeping the water warm for Amoulaki to come wash away the dust from her hair.

A Sunday in Beirut

In Beirut on good
Nights, I watch rockets fly
Over rooftops until my eyes hurt

Haas Mroue, *'Beirut Survivors Anonymous'*

A Sunday in Beirut

The rockets haven't stopped falling since six this morning. They first started in 1975, fifteen years ago, but we have had ceasefires now and then. There was a ceasefire just after the New Year, but it only lasted six days. That's when Dad made me come back here. I had been in Washington D.C. visiting my Mom like I do every holiday. This time I thought Dad would let me stay there considering how bad things have become here. But he sent a fax insisting that I return, saying that the schools will be reopening and that I promised to be with him for the last two years of high school.

Since I got back the shelling has been sporadic, no intense fighting. It usually flares up Friday afternoon, after the mosques quieten following the weekly prayers. By Sunday night it's usually calm again. I guess they don't want people going out on the weekends. Where would we go anyway? I don't remember the days before 1975 when Mom and Dad used to swim in the morning and ski in the afternoon. They told me that everyone called this dump of a city the Paris of the Middle East. Back then PAN AM alone had two 747 flights ever day from New York. Now when I fly to the States I have to transit in a hundred airports and I'm endlessly searched and questioned. I can't imagine this city as a tourist destination. Not with the tires burning on the streets, the humongous rats on the sidewalks and the checkpoints manned by guys younger than me.

It is noon on Sunday. It's sunny outside, but real windy. This past week they've been using a new kind of rocket. A Howitzer they called it on the news. One rocket can burn down a high-rise. We live in a six-storey building across from the American University. All morning Dad and I have been huddled in the corridor listening to the rockets. Every time one whistles overhead Dad lays the book he is reading on his lap. Our building shakes, the noise of shattered glass tumbling to the street as the rocket crashes somewhere else nearby. Dad lights his pipe and picks up his book again.

We are surrounded on three sides by tall buildings. On the kitchen side we face the Mediterranean. Sometimes late at night we can hear the waves. A faint smell of gunpowder and dust blows in through the broken windows. I use my teeth to open a bag of potato chips and quietly suck on them. I don't want to crunch too loudly and have Dad picking on me for eating too much.

I wonder where the last rocket crashed. I imagine fire raging now in an apartment. First the curtains burn, then the carpet and furniture. Maybe someone is injured, moaning quietly, cursing their bad luck. Some people (my cousins Tammy and Hoda, for example) think it is cowardly to go down to the shelter or hide in a corridor. They pretend nothing unusual is happening. They ignore the rockets to prove that the war has not conquered them yet. They sit in their living rooms sipping strong Turkish coffee and chain smoking. They eat in their kitchens and sleep on their beds (not in the corridor or shelter like us). They don't even listen to the news. They pop tranquilizers into their mouths and converse quietly about the latest Ungaro collection that was flown in from Milan and whether they will spend their summer vacation in Cannes, Dubrovnik or Palma. But I think really most of them are shit-scared because they all crack up in the end. The Valium they take must stop working. When finally there's a lull in the fighting they pack a small bag and run away somewhere far. Paris maybe, or Boston. Later we hear that they have become French or American residents and will never return. And I've seen them in those cities after they've run away. They stay glued to their televisions, waiting for the gory scenes from their country to appear on the evening news. As they sit watching the bodies being pulled out from under collapsed buildings, they nod to each other and light another cigarette. 'Thank God we got out in time,' they say, releasing the smoke through their noses. Later they go to Place Victor Hugo in the 16th arrondissement and sit in a café. They sip espresso and read about their country in *Le Figaro*. I see their kind every time Mom and I go to Paris.

It is three in the afternoon. It is calming down so there's no need to go to the shelter today. Dad sits in his black leather rocking chair reading a new book, a spy novel by John Le something. Dad teaches English literature at the University. For sixteen years he has taught the same classes. Two years ago he was offered a teaching job at Princeton. He refused. His mind must be warped or something. Doesn't he want to move on, to change? 'I can't function outside this city, Hani,' he says. 'I need the smell of garbage on the streets, the dark evenings by the candlelight and the rush of the rockets falling all around.' Rush? He's always so calm. I doubt sometimes if his heart ever pounds. He must have been interesting once for Mom to marry him. He was an assistant professor at Cornell for two years. Mom was his student and they fell in love - two displaced people in upstate New York. Mom told me it was snowing heavily in Ithaca the night I was born. The next day, Dad got an offer from the American University in Beirut to chair the English department. I was forty days old when we flew here, Mom said I cried all the way - and so did she. She didn't want to come back, she still had her thesis to write. But Dad convinced her and she still had some family here. So it was almost like coming back home - if there is such a thing.

I really didn't want to come back this time. But I had made a deal with Dad to get me out of that boarding school in Lausanne. I promised to live with him and go to school here if I could visit my Mom during vacations and go to a camp of my choice every summer. Dad doesn't like me spending too much time in the States. "You're becoming too Americanized," he tells me. Whatever that means.

"I was born there," I tell him, smiling.

"But I wasn't. And a son takes after his father."

"Mom is an American citizen, too"

"She wasn't when I married her," he had said without looking up from his book. "Anyway, if you so desperately yearn to reside in the land of ripped denim, be patient. In two years you'll be living there and will cherish these days in the Third World where your roots are, where your grandfather's bones lie and where your children's flesh should rot, eaten by ancient Third World worms."

Worms my ass. A typical talk with Dad. It always ends with him using his professor tone and making a final statement. I sit on the couch, across from him, watching him read. He always has such a stern look on his face. I bet he was a nerd in high school.

I don't hear any explosions or machine gun fire so it's pretty safe to go to my room. I fiddle with the new stereo that I carried back with me from the States. We only get six hours of electric power a day. I line up the record albums that I want to hear tonight at 9 p.m. when we get our share of the power rationing. Dire Straits albums mostly. I clean them, wiping them thoroughly with a special liquid that my cousin gave me in London. My Aunt Rebecca and her son, Loui, live in London. Every time I go to the States I get to stop over for a week to stay with them. Loui is my age and Aunt Rebecca is real fun. She even lets me smoke. "If you're going to smoke, you're going to smoke, so don't go stinking up my bathroom, smoke here where I can see you," she tells me. Dad doesn't like me going there much because Aunt Rebecca is Jewish. She's my mother's half sister. You see, back in 1934 my grandfather was interning at the American University Hospital. It was his last year of Med School and he fell in love with a nurse, who was a Spanish- Bulgarian Jew. His father threatened to disown him if he married her. "You're a Moslem," my great–grandfather told Grandpa, "you have to marry into your own faith." Of course Grandpa didn't listen and he married this nurse. She was called Rebecca and on a sultry August night she delivered a baby girl. But she, the mother, died two hours later of an internal haemorrhage. Aunt Rebecca inherited her mother's name, and according to my Dad, her mother's religion too. (Dad is so constipated sometimes, so intolerant). When Aunt Rebecca was six weeks old Grandpa, sick with grief, accepted to wed Frida, a Moslem. Frida had four children. One of them was my Mom. It's a long story, I can't remember it all and some parts are boring. Then Grandpa accepted a job in the middle of nowhere on the Palestine-Jordanian border. He was the only physician for miles and miles. That's where Mom spent her childhood until after Israel started existing and things got worse and she was sent to boarding school in Cairo.

It's almost 8 p. m. I can listen to my albums soon. I go to the kitchen and open a can of baked beans. I eat from the pan, using a large wooden spoon, like the cowboys do in all the Westerns. Dad is still reading by the candlelight. He hasn't talked much today, but that's not unusual. "Dad, do you want to eat something?" I call out.

"No Hani, I'm not hungry. But you better eat those Big Macs you carried back with you from D.C. You know the freezer doesn't work properly without the power."

"Okay, Okay, I'll eat them."

He has been bugging me about those burgers ever since I got back. I'll show him. I get up and reach for the three soggy buns from the warm fridge and start shovelling them down my throat. Literally. I eat all three in less than two minutes. Last year at Camp in Santa Barbara I won the chocolate cake eating contest. I ate six slices in three minutes. My art of wolfing is perfected thanks to these boring Beirut evenings.

When I'm with Mom I never get the urge to binge. "Compulsive eating disorder," Grandpa had told Mom, "that's my diagnosis." Mom told me to ignore him. She knew I could control my eating and it was only out of spite for Dad and this city that I did it. She said that she'd do the same if she was forced to live here again. Mom left in 1975 and took me with her to New York. She went back to school, to Columbia, and I went to kindergarten. When I turned six Dad insisted that I go to a boarding school of his choice, 'I don't want my boy speaking with a Brooklyn accent,' he wrote my Mom in a letter that I later found. Mom accepted because she was broke and she wanted me to get a good education. She never went back to Dad. He stayed in Beirut all alone and I went to school in Switzerland. It was there that I started getting these weird feelings that make me want to eat until I throw up. I get these feelings when I'm in this city and around Dad. It's like being in a straitjacket and I'm squirming and eating and eating. Then I can't rest until I've released the thick, yellow paste into the toilet bowl. I like that feeling when the liquid rises to my throat, my nose runs and my stomach heaves. Afterward I feel relieved and I can sleep. I never get these feelings around Mom. She always has things to tell me. She listens to me. She gives me acrylics and a canvas and she plays Orff's Carmina Burana on her CD at full blast and orders me to start painting. Mom works for the World Bank, but is a painter too.

The lights come on suddenly and I jump from my bed. It's past 9 p.m. I must have dozed off. I can hear Dad fixing himself a drink in the kitchen. I listen to my favourite song- Brothers in Arms - and try not to think of school tomorrow. I still have some Geometry homework to do. Maybe a few rockets will crash nearby tonight, then they'll cancel morning classes. We are only thirty students in the whole high school. It's a special school for foreigners. State Department brats left last year after the U.S. Embassy blew up. We were sitting in Art class and suddenly dust started falling from the ceiling, doors blew open and my ears hurt. A few minutes later we saw the smoke billowing from the Embassy building four blocks down the street. Two of my classmates' fathers were killed. Mrs Lockwood, our English teacher, was at the Embassy at the time and she was blinded. We all went to the hospital the next day. I never had to read the poem by Wordsworth out loud. The bomb saved my life. But I did feel sad for Mrs Lockwood. A few weeks later, helicopters evacuated all the Embassy dependents and our school shrank in size. As it turned out Mrs Lockwood regained some of her eyesight. I sent her a card for Christmas.

I can't complain about this school, though. It's better than boarding school. I hate to remember those long years in Switzerland, my heart starts to pound. All the students were such snobs, their parents millionaires. They called me 'Le petit Arab,' because I have black hair and my name is not French or German or American. "I'm not an Arab," I would shout.

"What are you then?" They would ask.

"I don't know. But I'm not an Arab," I would respond, tears flooding down my eyes. Slowly I learnt a new trick. I omitted the last vowel of my name and replaced it with an s. I became Hans. I would practice my German every night. When they moved me to a new boarding house, most of the students were new and I was known as Hans. When someone called me Hani, I would pretend that that had been a nickname. "My real name is Hans," I would say, touching them lightly on the shoulder and looking straight into their eyes. No one called me an Arab again. With my dark hair I did not look like a Northern European. But I enjoyed that ambiguity. I still do. "My ancestors were from Naples," I say. Everyone likes Italians. Why should anyone have the pleasure of classifying me, or calling me an Arab or an American? When people ask me where I'm from I say, "everywhere and nowhere." Once in the metro in Paris a French kid was scribbling graffiti on the wall. 'Dirty Arab, Dirty Jew,' he wrote, using red paint. I couldn't sleep that night. I called Aunt Rebecca. "Hey what are you so upset about?" She said. "It's statistically proven that the French use the least soap and toothpaste among the world's population. They're the dirty ones and don't you forget that."

Dad shuffles into bed just twenty minutes after the power comes back on. I lower the volume on my stereo and strip off my clothes. I lie in my underwear on my bed. The light bothers me so I turn it off. I'm so used to the dark now. I hear Dad coughing from his bedroom. I wonder what he thinks about at night. Does he have any desires left? I've never seen him with a woman. I wonder if he has a girlfriend in Munich. That's where he spent his Christmas vacation, researching his book, something about German writers. I asked him what he did. "I wrote, Hani. Then I was in a Thomas Mann mood and took the train down to Venice," he said. Whatever that means. He never talks to me about girls or sex or anything. It's like sex doesn't even exist for him. I was able to get into a sex shop in D.C. with a fake I.D. I couldn't believe all those magazines, hundreds of them. I was so nervous I could hardly pick one up. There were so many men Dad's age browsing, buying blue videos. They looked normal, almost too well dressed, like the types that sit Business Class on the London-Dulles British Airways flights. I had thought only perverts walked into such places. I didn't tell anyone but Loui that I went. He gave me a hard time for not buying him a magazine.

I got up to take a piss, careful not to aim for the middle so as to not make too much noise and wake up Dad. I grab a wad of toilet paper. Lying on my bed in the dark I think of Claudia, the Venezuelan girl that was with me at camp last summer. She's naked on the beach and I have all my clothes on. For some reason I'm wearing a suit and a tie. She puts her head between my legs and I caress her tanned back and fondle her pointed nipples.

I stuff the wet toilet paper in my book bag. I wouldn't want Dad seeing it in the morning when he comes into my room to wake me up. It would embarrass him, I know. Insomnia has hit me tonight and I toss and turn in my bed. I listen to some Christmas carols. When I was a kid in Brooklyn I used to hate the weeks after Christmas; no one played Christmas carols. We had to throw out our tree. "But why can't we keep it forever?" I would ask my Mom.

"Look, everyone is throwing out their tree, too." And sure enough, after New Years, the sidewalks would be lined with used Christmas trees. I would touch each one gently not comprehending why the fun of Christmas had to be over. Then school would start and I would forget about my tree until the following year.

I get a funny taste in my mouth and turn off my stereo. Maybe there is something biological about not being able to listen to Christmas carols in January. This Christmas Mom really surprised me. She bought airline tickets to Prague. "For Easter we'll meet in Czechoslovakia Hanis." (She calls me Hanis. She says Hans is too German and Hani reminds her of her abandoned country.) "I want to be in a county full of positive vibes," she had said excitedly. She bought all of Vaclav Havel's plays and spent New Year's Eve reading them. That night I heard her sobbing in her room. The walls are thin in her apartment. The next morning, when I asked her what was wrong, it took her a while to answer. "I really don't know why I was crying Hanis. I felt jealous and sad. I was thinking of Prague and feeling real jealousy for the first time in my life. I wanted to be among those people who suddenly got what they've always wanted. And I felt angry because we don't have a man like Vaclav Havel to take care of us."

Mom has been depressed lately. Her boyfriend for the past eight years died in a motorcycle accident last summer. She hasn't been the same since. I liked the guy a lot. We spent many vacations with him in his home near Portofino. Of course Dad doesn't know a thing. He wouldn't have approved of me riding on a motorcycle with his ex-wife's boyfriend.

It's 2 a.m. I listen to the news hoping it hasn't calmed down so I won't have to go to school. But it has. There are only some reports of sniping on the Green Line. Two killed. Nothing major. The city will be normal tomorrow and I have to get up early and solve these Geometry problems. In an hour they'll cut off the power again. I go to the kitchen and eat a banana. Then some peanuts. In the living room I do fifteen push-ups and fifty sit-ups. It is real quiet outside. Anytime now the *Muezzin* from the mosque down the street will start screeching the morning prayers into the loudspeakers. They've added so much power to those speakers lately. Somewhere out there, between the buildings and the mosques, in some cold basement, Uncle Terry is held hostage. He was the Dean at the University. He used to be over at our house all the time. He and Dad used to sit around discussing books for hours. I saw a video of him in the States. He looked funny with a beard.

I go out on the kitchen balcony hoping to hear the waves. I stand there half naked, shivering. I'm a prisoner here. The streetlights along the *Corniche* flicker and go out. The city is plunged into darkness again. I live for Spring break in Prague. I close my eyes and sway with the wind. I live for summer camp in California. I hear a wave. I see Claudia on a surfboard and me sitting on the warm sand watching the other surfers looking at Claudia's boobs as they roll with the wave

Sixteen Years of Dust

We lived a war with no name
and escaped. We now belong to a culture
That has no name.

Haas Mroue, *'Beirut Survivors Anonymous'*

Sixteen Years of Dust

Lara Cusa left Beirut in the summer of 1975, just a few months after the civil war began. She thought she was leaving for a couple of weeks, that things would calm down and she would return. But the war only got worse and she enrolled in film school in Paris. She lived by the radio, listening to news of the war: the hotel wars, black Saturday, kidnappings and murders. She spent hours trying to call her mother in Beirut. She felt guilty at having left her mother and sister alone. She'd stand by the *École Militaire* waiting for the bus in the early morning drizzle and think of getting on the next plane to Beirut. But she couldn't bear the idea of the empty plane, the landing at Beirut airport, the questions about her religion, the smoke rising from buildings, and the detours to avoid flying roadblocks from the airport to their house. She'd get on the bus and head for her class where she'd sit, dazed, listening to the rockets falling in her head.

Now, Lara Cusa is sitting in her *Le Club* seat on an Air France Air bus heading for Nice. She is sipping champagne and looking out the window at the Alps below her. She is thinking about the mountains of her homeland, the rounded mountain tops with their dry shrubs and views of the Mediterranean, the mountains of Lebanon. She can almost smell the fresh milk curd, the wax and honey. These mountains seem crude, she thinks, unfriendly, almost ferocious in their jaggedness, landlocked hundreds of miles from the sea. Lara Cusa is used to flying. But lately she's been flying Business Class. Her latest film, *Sixteen Years of Dust*, has been invited to the Cannes Film Festival, where she is now heading.

As the plane descends into Nice, Lara sees the Mediterranean and sighs. Her heart cramps at the pine forest below, the tiny islands, the blue sea. She had been elated when her sister, Mona, wrote to tell her that she would come to Paris with Claude to get married. It was January 1976. Lara cleaned her apartment, cooked dinner and then went to the airports to meet Claude and Mona. She watched the passengers disembark. She thought they looked defeated, as if they had lost a loved one, their eyes lowered to the ground, their smiles forced. She waited for three hours and still her sister hadn't shown up. Lara went home and drank a bottle of Beaujolais and ate a kilo of sautéed endives with roquefort sauce.

After she heard the news of Mona's death by a sniper bullet, Lara vowed never to return to her country of birth. She decided to use the war. She wanted to make money out of it. She wanted to milk the idea that her country was embroiled in civil war. She began making short films for one of the TV stations in Paris. She'd take her camera to Fouquet's, Carette and Le Garage and film the Lebanese women wrapped in fur coats in May, delicately chewing on chocolate éclairs, sipping espresso or dancing to the latest Abba songs. She'd juxtapose these images with footage of the civil war that was sent from Beirut. She was ridiculed by the rich Lebanese community in Paris. But she didn't stop. She'd interview maids that worked for rich Lebanese businessmen. One maid confessed to having been raped several times by her employer. Another said that her employer threatened to kill her when she accidentally stumbled upon a suitcase filled with hashish. The documentary, entitled *Civil War on Ave. Victor Hugo*, was invited to the East German Film Festival in Leipzig, where it won third place.

When Lara Cusa walks down the steps at Nice airport and smells the humid air mixed with the salty smell of the sea, she is overcome by a deep sadness. The air reminds her so much of Beirut. This is what I need, she thinks to herself, warm breezes, palm trees and long walks by the sea.

After collecting her bags, she heads for the festival booth where she is escorted into a brand new Renault 25 with black leather seats. The festival flag flies over the antenna and as the car merges into the fast lane heading to Cannes, Lara presses the button to open her window. The warm air makes her hair fly and Lara decides that she will leave Paris very soon and live somewhere warm.

Her film is not scheduled to be shown until the following day, but Lara has received several invitations to parties, all being held tonight. After checking in at the Carlton and unpacking, she goes through the invitations. A rich Lebanese artist is having a dinner party at his villa in Mougins; a producer from Warner Brothers is having a poolside party at the Martinez; a British director is having an all-directors party on his yacht; Madonna's party is at the Hôtel du Cap; and a distributor for Orion is having a cocktail party at the Palm Beach.

Lara goes out on the balcony in Cannes, she can hear the music drifting down from the Palais des Festival. Tomorrow she will be escorted at eight o'clock to the official screening of her film. Her crew will be there and a few of her friends are flying down from Paris for the occasion. George had called, wanting to escort her, but she refused. She can't face him until her film is bought by a distributor. She wants to write him a cheque while he looks on. She will write *One Million and No Cents* and blow smoke in his face from her cigar.

After Lara showers, she sees a hair on her chin which she plucks with tweezers. She notices the hair on her arms is dark again and she get out her dye kit and patiently dabs both her arms in the yellow colored paint. She decides to go to the Orion cocktail party and suck up to the distributor who just might invite her to Los Angeles. Then she will go up to Mougins to the party of the Beiruti artist. She had met the painter a few times and had been intrigued by his detachment from their land of origin. A good sign, thinks Lara as she zips up her black mini-skirt.

Walter Cohen greets her warmly when she enters the cocktail party.
"I've heard so much about your film," he says.
Lara smiles, looks around for the champagne. "I hear people in America don't care about Beirut now that the Marines have withdrawn and the hostages are out," Lara says. She is irritated by the uncolorful mood of the

party, irritated at the grey suit that Cohen is wearing. This is Cannes, she wants to tell him, not Burbank at noon. Cohen starts to mumble things about the American public, the recession.

"We at Orion are committed to foreign films, to showing Americans the cream of what is made overseas," he is saying.

A waiter passes with a tray of champagne glasses and Lara takes two. "The cream?" She says. She feels like making an impression tonight. She feels sexy and dangerous and slightly buzzed from all the attention.

"What is your film about, Lara?" asks Cohen, gently taking an empty champagne glass from her hand and handing it to a passing waiter.

"My film is about war immigrants," Lara says. The champagne has gone to her head and she is enjoying Cohen's eyes on her cleavage. "Hundreds of thousands of people fled the country when the civil war began sixteen years ago. The rich, the poor, the smugglers, the pimps and the whores. But they all have one thing in common. Each of them has had a loved one killed or kidnapped or maimed and all of them carry this around with them. They can't run away from it, wherever they go. And what has this war accomplished, you may ask, Mr Cohen? Nothing. Sixteen years for nothing, just the country crumbling to dust."

Cohen stifles a yawn. Lara realises that she is talking too much, that she might lose Cohen's interest. What short concentration spans those Hollywood people have, thinks Lara.

Back in the Renault heading up the hill to Mougins, Lara is thankful she is going to Nadim's party. She likes to be surrounded by people who know what it is to have civil war ravage a city. Lara feels good. Cohen has given her enough hints that he is willing to distribute her film. They will sign the contract the day after her screening. I can work in Hollywood now, thinks Lara. She flips open her pocket mirror and dabs her lips with red lipstick as the car pulls up to the gates of a hillside mansion.

Nadim and about twelve other people are standing around the barbecue by the swimming pool. Nadim hugs her. She recognizes a few faces - a French actor, a Moroccan director, an Egyptian singer.

"Ladies and gentlemen," Nadim says, holding up his champagne glass, "our one and only Lara Cusa."

"Nadim, stop it," Lara hisses, turning red in the face.

Lara notices the cicadas humming in the background, the bougainvillea by the steps, the smell of orange blossoms from the nearby orchard.

"Now Zeinab will dance for us," Nadim says. And a woman dressed in black from head to toe, her face covered gypsy-style with a black shawl, starts belly dancing around the swimming pool. The pool is lit and there's smoke and the smell of charred meat coming from the stone barbecue. Someone is playing the *oud*. Nadim gets Lara a glass of champagne. He takes out a little vial of white powder and as they stand in the warm evening breeze, the cicadas humming in the background and Zeinab dancing to a sad melody, Nadim snorts some coke and asks Lara if she wants some. She shakes her head, her eyes on Zeinab, the delicate hand movements, the waist rotating ever so slightly to the music. If only she could dance like that, express her emotions in a movement of a limb, or a muscle or a body part. Lara knows that Cohen will treat her well, will probably arrange the financing for her next film. She will stay at the Bel Age on Sunset and invite him for a drink. She will not ask about his wife. She will take him to the rooftop pool and ask him to show her L.A. She will take out her breasts in the cool breeze on the roof of the Bel Age and ask Cohen if he wants to hold them. She will mould the film to suit his tastes, the tastes of the American public. She's changed in sixteen years. She wants many things to make up for a lost country, a lost sister. She wants to leave Paris. Sixteen years is a long time. She wants to have her own villa, to throw parties, and have her own orange grove. She wants a cook and a driver and a Saab convertible. She wants to hire dancers and throw parties and have parking attendants valet her guests' cars.

The dancing has finished and Lara watches as Zeinab takes off the shawl and mask to reveal a thin, manly face. Then Zeinab speaks and Lara realises that it is a man, a female impersonator, a male belly dancer. Lara looks around for Nadim to ask for more champagne, but he's disappeared. Zeinab or whatever his name is walks up to her, all sweaty, his chest heaving from dancing.

"My real name is Walid," he says holding out his hand. "Would you have me in one of your films?" He is tall and she has to tilt her head slightly upward to look at him. Lara notices again how thin his face is. She tries not to stare.

"Sure, if I make another film," she says looking away. "I don't know what's going to happen tomorrow, it might be a flop."

He looks at her and smiles and Lara feels like shouting CUT, to move on to the next scene. He is making her uncomfortable. Why would a man want to belly dance? Why would a *woman* want to belly dance in public, Lara has always asked herself.

"I'm going to be in Madonna's next music video," he says. "Are you going to her party later on?"

Lara notices that the hairs on his arm are blonde. She wants to ask him what he uses, paste or spray? She wants to ask him if he has AIDS.

"I'm going to bed soon," says Lara taking a few steps backwards, looking away. "I have a big day tomorrow."

"I'll send my resume to your producer in Paris," he says and walks off.

Lara suddenly notices that the music has stopped, and the cicadas are really loud and that she is irritated by the noise. She's irritated by that man, that dance. He's so comfortable, she thinks, uninhibited. Even at nightclubs Lara cannot dance. She drinks too much and wobbles around. At work, she hides behind the camera, her notepad her clipboard. Lara Cusa walks slowly around the garden towards the gates where the R25 is parked. The driver is leaning against the front of the car, smoking. She asks him for a cigarette and then gets into the back seat and once again rolls down the window and lets her hair fly as they head down the hill toward Cannes.

Lara is nervous. She can feel her stomach tightening, her mouth drying. Tomorrow is her big day. It will be long and festive: the short drive from the Carlton in a darkened limo, the cameras flashing as she climbs the stairs of the Palais. She will turn and wave. The applause will be minimal since no one really knows who she is - a Third World director with phoney blonde hair and an artificially small nose. Then the screening of her film - she will grimace at every cut, worry about the soundtrack and the color. Then the applause, the kissing, the champagne, the interviews, the photographs.

The phone will ring for two days. Then the flowers and the smiles will slowly diminish when the winning films are selected and hers is not one of them. Then the plane ride back to Paris, to her two-room apartment, dark and humid, and her friends and meetings and talk of another film and waiting for Orion to call. She will move to Los Angeles. She will get nowhere in Paris. In Paris only the stars get to valet park. In Los Angeles anyone with three dollars can valet park. She will sign a contract with a studio to direct a film on Terry Anderson and the hostages. She will rent a house with a pool, get a dog, maybe send for her mother to come from Beirut for a while, cook for her.

As the car speeds down Boulevard Carnot, Lara thinks that directors are stars only for a day or two a year, when their film is playing in some festival. Today she is a star. She could pull up at the Hôtel du Cap and would not be turned away. She could go to Madonna's party, show the material girl her legs in black stockings. Maybe Zeinab could teach her to dance and Madonna would have her direct one of her videos.

Yes, Lara will definitely move to Los Angeles. She will direct a film on the hostages. Maybe in a few years she could make a film on the Marine experience in Beirut, maybe a love story about a young Lebanese girl falling in love with a Marine. The Marine leaves in the end. They always do. And the girl from the Third World would be left to cook for her bearded brothers and cut fresh flowers for her mother's grave. Lara Cusa knows the only way out, the only way to achieve fame and afford a house with a swimming pool, would be to use the war. Maybe she would do some acting, she thinks, play the mistress of a *Mossad Katsa.*

The traffic is heavy, even at midnight, and the driver has to make a detour to get to the Carlton. Lara is thinking of her sister Mona. Even if Lara moves to Los Angeles she will remember Mona every day.

How many times has she pictured the scene in her mind, shot it from different angles.

Scene: Mona's death. A crane shot of the car crossing the bridge, cut to an extreme close–up the moment the bullet enters Mona's neck, blood spurting, cut back to the sniper sitting back, reloading his rifle, cut to Mona letting go of the wheel, losing control of the car, cut to external shot of the red VW rolling over the Ring Bridge (voice-over: Claude moaning), cut to endives with roquefort sauce, a bottle of Beaujolais, Lara sprawled out on her bed, cut to the red VW, under the bridge, crushed, blood dripping from the driver's door into the dust.

Fade to black.

Running on Wind

No one has the answers. We all find ways to cope.

Haas Mroue, *'Days of War'*

Crumpton Hud

Running on Wind

Midnight. I am lying in bed in our big house, too big a house to live in without memories. I haven't taken my valium today, yet my body feels heavy, my 99-pound body buried under these sheets.

Hani works late at the refinery and when he comes home, just before midnight, I am too tired to sit with him. So he eats his dinner alone watching TV in the living room.

The air conditioning has been on since mid- March. Now it is the first day of August. How much longer can I last in this humid country? I think of my children. I see their faces. Faces of the children I have yet to give birth to. Their voices fill the long nights I spend in this bed waiting. I hear them calling to me from beneath the rubble of the apartment building we once lived in. "Mama, Mama," their voices whisper in my ear. The air conditioning hums in my brain. Kuwait is not a place to raise kids. Maybe one day when we live in another country I will have children.

I can hear the television and the sound of Hani chewing the rice and okra stew I cooked for him. The Egyptian grocer delivers fresh okra from Egypt right to my door. Hani takes me shopping on Friday afternoons after he has slept for fifteen hours. But he rushes me in the supermarket and I am not able to shop properly. "You're so slow," he tells me as I pick cucumbers or tomatoes. "Today's my only day off and I have to stand here waiting for you."

Hani has finished eating. He is watching an Indian movie and there's lots of screaming. Once I asked him not to turn up the volume on the TV so loud, that I needed to sleep.

"You'll sleep all day," he said, "it won't hurt you not to sleep at night."

I didn't use to sleep all day. When my sister came from America she told me to find a hobby. "Housewives don't sleep all day in America," she said. "Find something to do apart from the cooking and the cleaning." She bought me watercolors and a brush and taught me how to use them. Hani assumed it was my sister who was painting and I did not tell him otherwise. After my sister went back to Philadelphia I would paint in the morning, while Hani was at work. But one day I got paint on the new beige carpet and Hani saw it, a big blue spot right there in the living room. "What is this you do while I'm away, playing with the paint like a retarded child?" he said, as he flipped channels on the TV.

I didn't dare paint again. I didn't want him to think that my sister had a bad influence on me. But I think he does. When I asked to visit her, he refused. "We can't afford it," he said. "You wanted a new carpet. I got it for you. You wanted a new fridge. I got it for you. America is too far away and expensive. Besides, it's dangerous for you there. You'd get lost."

So now I sleep. I take my valium every day and sometimes my neighbor, Jeannette, slips me a few ecstasy pills which she gets through her psychiatrist in Paris. I do crazy things when I take those pills. I stand in front of a mirror in my bedroom, naked. We never had a mirror in the bathroom when I was growing up. And the house was always full of people: aunts, uncles, brothers. I was never alone to be able to stand naked in front of a mirror. Now whenever I take those pills I look at myself and touch my body lightly.

Hani never touches me. He gets inside of me sometimes and I breathe quicker. I tell him not to but he doesn't listen. If only he would touch me first, like he used to. When he rolls off me, already asleep and snoring, I watch him. I know I don't please him. He says I'm useless because I can't have children. My gynaecologist explained to us about low sperm counts after we were both examined. But Hani never listens. "What would that woman know anyway?" he tells me when I argue with him. "She doesn't look like a doctor. She has blonde hair."

And I sleep. The air conditioning is buzzing in my brain and I get up, my head spinning, and turn it off and open the windows. The humid air seeps in and I close my eyes and lie back down on the bed. With no valium in my blood, my brain is alive and I remember what I never want to remember. Those Israeli F-16s circling endlessly in the still, green air and Hani and I running. Running away from another war. We had been married four years and Hani loved me. He held me all the way to Damascus. I was weeping, forced to abandon my home and run away from the jets and the phosphorous shells. As we ran I felt a warm feeling between my legs, liquid trickling all the way to my ankles. My baby. I lost my baby, a clump of blood, on the loose gravel just outside Damascus.

The noise of the jets, the tanks and machine guns and the blood had drowned everything but my love for Hani. And with his arms around me we came here and started a new life. Hani found a good position at the refinery and soon he had two hundred men under his command. He started making more money than he'd ever seen and he drifted away from me. And I started sleeping.

I am sweating. I can't seem to move my body. It has suddenly gone limp.

And Hani still watches TV.

Eight years ago, as we fled the Israeli invasion, I could have been stripped of my flesh by a phosphorus shell and still Hani would have loved me. Now he doesn't even look at me. I know I have blue circles around my eyes, and my thighs have doubled in size. But once he loved me.

When that rocket crashed into our apartment and everything sizzled from the heat of the phosphorus, Hani held me to his chest and we prayed together. Then the soldiers came and helped us down the ladder to the street. We ran away from our burning building. Another rocket crashed into it and the building burned until it collapsed. And I wanted to be there, in my apartment. I wanted the roof to collapse over me. I wanted to be buried under the pile of rubble, the rubble of my building. I wanted to taste my own blood, to see my skin sizzling and peeling from a phosphorus shell. I stayed in the hospital in Damascus. I thought I would never come out. But Hani held my hand until these thoughts evaporated from my mind and we came to Kuwait and started a new life.

I am all wet. The temperature outside must be 103 degrees. It doesn't get cooler here at night. The air smells of rotten fish and kerosene. Hani's snoring is louder than the television. I get up and turn the air conditioning back on. I close the windows. I drag myself into the living room. My thin cotton nightgown seems to crush me with its weight. I take Hani's empty plate to the kitchen, then I lean against the dining room table and from a distance watch Hani sleeping. He twitches his nose every few minutes and his eyelashes tremble slightly. When he sleeps he looks like the Hani I knew when we were first married. Now that he's gone most of the day, Jeannette brings me pizza sometimes from the Pizza Hut that just opened downtown. And we watch videos, soap operas from America. Hani doesn't approve of me going anywhere with Jeannette so we stay home. I always have to tell Jeannette to leave before Hani comes. "She's a rich lady and I don't want her in my house," Hani has told me many times. He knows she's my only friend.

I watch Hani for a long time, until I hear a faint rumble far away. It doesn't rain here in the summer. I look out the living room window. The street lights have been turned off. I slide my damp body onto the couch and sit next to Hani and close my eyes.

I see a little girl of fifteen, wet from the rain, weeping in an orange grove after losing her dolls while fleeing Palestine. "Soraya, Soraya," my father is calling out for me and I do not answer. But he finds me and holds my hand and we walk for two days until we reach Tyre.

"I'll get you new dolls when we have a home again," my father tells me. And we make a home out of a stone house with a tin roof. But my father forgets about my dolls and when I cry he is distracted, playing with his worry beads. And he forgets to hold my hand.

Hani stirs. The rumble is getting closer.

I keep my eyes closed. I see a little girl of thirty five, weeping, Hani holding her hand, as they flee Tyre, the Merkava tanks rumbling ominously behind them. "We'll make a new home, I promise you, Soraya," he says to me. "We'll have children and I'll buy you anything you want."

An explosion very far away. Hani still snores. If I hadn't been through two or three wars I would have thought it was a door banging. The sound is comforting. It reminds me of Haifa. And Tyre. It reminds me of home. The rumbling is getting louder, the noise of hundreds of tanks. I reach for the shortwave and put it to my ear. Iraq is invading us.

Peace. I put my head on Hani's chest and listen to his breathing. Soon we'll have to run again.

Occupation: Photojournalist

I want to use Adam and Eve as my parachute
glide down with a billion loaves of bread
dipped in honey
and apples
and then stab both Adam and Eve in the groin
and drench my disfigured face with their translucent blood.

Haas Mroue, *'Current Affairs'*

Occupation: Photojournalist

The noise inside the airplane was very loud as it made its final approach into Borja airport. Just a few more minutes, thought Guy to himself, as he looked out from his little window. All he could see was miles of sand. He noticed how the passengers were quiet, not the usual chatter of people returning home. He turned and looked at the man sitting next to him. His face seemed pale, his eyes were red, drained of all energy. All the men wore loose shirts and baggy trousers the color of the sand. The women wore somewhat darker pieces of cloths wrapped around their bodies.

The D.C. 3 touched down with a thump, and taxied quickly to a small box-like building. The passengers got up sluggishly and collected their bags. They all were carrying huge bags bulging with food, flour, rice, sugar and potatoes. They were all silent, as though they were nearing a prison and not going home.

Guy followed the other passengers onto the staircase of the plane. A gust of hot wind blew some sand into his face. He had not prepared himself mentally for this kind of heat. He had rushed so quickly to the airport, wanting to be the first to uncover the horror of the famine to the world. As Guy slowly descended the stairs his clothes suddenly turned wet from humidity and the mosquitoes hovered around him. In this part of the world, the heat persists even at night. Even though Guy had been in Borja for only a few minutes, he longed for home, for the moment when he would leave this hot, scalding world. He stood in line for the passport control, his heart beating fast. Perspiration streamed down the sides of his face as his turn neared. Guy looked around and realized that he was the only foreigner. Borja embassies around the world had stopped issuing visas to any foreigners after rumours of a famine had leaked out only a few days before. Guy had to be smart enough so that he would be given a visa, even if just a transit one for a few days. His hands shook uncontrollably as he clutched his passport tightly. This was Guy's first trip as a photojournalist.

"Passport," demanded the passport officer. Guy handed him the passport, wet from his sweaty hands. The officer flipped through it once trying to find the visa. He then went back to the first page, where Guy's photograph was. "Is you?" he asked, pointing to the photo.

"Yes," answered Guy quietly. Who else could it be? He tried smiling at the officer to hide the nervousness he felt.

"Show me visa," the officer demanded.

As Guy, his hands shaking, began fumbling with the passport, a woman standing in line behind Guy, began screaming. She was an elderly woman, and had accidentally dropped the sack of potatoes that she was carrying. The potatoes had rolled all over the floor, and people were frantically trying to get their share. The passport officer grabbed Guy's passport and stamped it on a blank page.

"Go! Go!" he screamed at Guy. He then got up and started picking up the potatoes that were around him. Guy moved on and found his bag. The heat was intense in the crowded airport as he stood in line for customs clearance. There was only one officer searching all the passengers. His moustache almost reached his ears, he was thin and short and capable of being malicious. What bothered Guy was that he was the only foreigner, and they did not seem to like foreigners.

"Passport," demanded the custom officer, looking at Guy closely. He studied the passport for a minute, hesitating at the photograph. He then pointed to Guy's bag. "What is there?"

"Camera, clothes…"

"Hashish?" asked the customs officer.

"No. Camera, Cam-era," replied Guy slowly.

"Where Hashish?"

"No hashish," Guy responded looking directly into his eyes.

"No hashish, no hashish," muttered the officer slowly as he searched the rest of the contents uninterested and then motioned to Guy to take his bag and leave.

Guy walked out into the dreadful sunlight and looked for a taxi. He got into the back seat and told the sleepy driver to take him to the Hilton. The driver started the engine reluctantly, as though he was content to have stayed slumped in his seat in the heat. He looked at Guy in his mirror. Guy looked back. Most taxi drivers were secret service, and almost everyone in this country was secret service, too.

"You newspaper man?" he asked Guy.

Guy nodded. The driver would not understand "Freelance photojournalist".

"Many people here hungry, you know?"

Guy nodded again. He would not be here if he did not know.

"Many people die, and your people know about it nothing," the driver continued. Guy hesitated to tell him that if *his* people would give visas, then maybe the world would know about it. The taxi pulled up in front of a tall, dirty building. Guy did not understand why they had stopped. "You no want Hilton? This Hilton," the driver said impatiently. Guy looked again at the dirty building, paid the driver and entered.

It was not that bad inside. There was no electricity, therefore no air-conditioning. It was once a fashionable hotel, when the country was not so poor. Guy asked the receptionist about the reservation.

"Passport," he demanded.

"Why do you want the passport?" asked Guy innocently.

"It's a formality."

Guy handed him the passport.

"I'll keep it for a while," the receptionist said shrewdly.

Guy said nothing. He was handed a form full of questions about his occupation and reasons for being in this country. Guy labored to look innocent as the receptionist eyed him silently. He was innocent now, but not for long. When he uncovered the reality of famine to the world, he would be more than guilty and very famous.

"How long are you staying?" he snapped at Guy.

"Long enough to plan my trip south," Guy answered glaring back at him. Interrogation was not exactly the job of the receptionist. Guy picked his bag and left him, ready to attack with another question.

Guy entered the dark room and lit the candle. He took it to the bathroom and opened the water tap. Brown water flowed out. He washed his face and looked in the mirror. His unshaven face was pale, and his eyes had big circles under them. Guy was exhausted from the long flight, but anxiety bid him have a cup of coffee and plan the next few days. He put on fresh clothes and left the hotel under the suspicious eye of the receptionist.

The mosquitoes attacked him once again. Although it was late afternoon, the heat had not subsided. Guy looked around him: the streets were full of lethargic people walking slowly, aimlessly. Despite the crowd, all was quiet.

The people were too tired, too hot to speak. They seemed to talk with their eyes, because speaking would mean wasting precious energy. Guy walked around for a while studying their movements. They all looked the same. He could not find a place to have coffee, so he turned back in the direction of the hotel.

Guy was alone in the huge coffee shop of the hotel. He signalled to the waiter, who was obviously bored.

"Coffee, please," he requested

The waiter's eyes opened wide.

"No coffee."

Guy looked at him closely.

"Tea?"

"No tea."

"Water?"

The waiter's eyes narrowed down as he smiled. He got Guy a glass of warm brown water.

"Eat?" he asked Guy innocently.

Guy nodded, curious to see the menu. There was nobody else in the hotel. Any other journalist would stay at the Hilton, too. But Guy was alone; there was no-one.

The waiter returned slowly carrying a tray with two plates.

Guy stared at the dishes as he placed them on the table. One was full of plain white rice, the other dry noodles. A piece of stale bread sat between them. He had not imagined that it would be this bad. He ate slowly, forcing the dry starch down his throat and began planning his trip to the famine-stricken area. He had to leave soon. After dinner, Guy went directly to the receptionist.

"Where can I rent a jeep?" he asked him.

"When do you want it?"

"Tomorrow at dawn."

"Okay," said the receptionist.

"Can I have my passport back?" asked Guy timidly.

"Tomorrow."

Guy reached for his nearly empty flask of water. It needed to last him until evening. Ever since he had left the city just before dawn he had seen nothing but endless sand dunes and the scorching sunlight. Guy was driving his jeep, heading south. In a few hours, he expected to reach the area where there had been no rain for years, and where it was said eighty people died every day. If he could only get the right photographs, he would rush back to the airport and head for home. In the distance, he saw several black figures moving slowly. As he approached them, Guy realized that they were a family walking silently under the hot sun. When he stopped the engine, not a sound could be heard. The mother, father and five children wore only small pieces of cloth wrapped loosely around their bodies. Their eyes moved slowly, staring at Guy. They looked dead. There was no recognition, no reflection in their black eyes. Their skin was dry, cracks were visible all over their bodies. He could count the ribs in their chests. The youngest child, about three years old, had an incredibly inflated stomach. His death must be near. The father suddenly put his hand to his mouth, a sign signifying food. Should he give them what he had? They were probably walking north in the hope of finding food. He remembered that he was not here to be a relief worker. He reached for his camera, but did not pick it up. The picture could make him famous, yet Guy was paralyzed. Can he just take a picture and move on? Could a photographer be so cruel?

He stared from the camera to the family. Realizing that he would be of no help, they resumed their slow shuffle northwards. Guy stood for a few minutes clutching his camera tightly. He looked again at the family, who were walking slowly away from him. Suddenly, he released the camera and picked up the box of food and his flask of water and ran after the family. They turned around slowly, their black eyes unblinking as he approached them. Guy placed the box of food on the sand in front of them and ran back to the jeep. He started the motor and drove off. He did not want to look back.

The sun was high in the sky as Guy drove farther south. Families like the one he had encountered earlier filled the desert. They were all walking northwards. They had nothing with them. Their belongings meant nothing to them now. Their only care was to live, or try to live. Every few minutes, Guy would pass a corpse of a baby or an old person lying majestically on the sand, their souls having surrendered to the sun. They had died in search of life's basic necessity; good. Now they were united with the sun and sand. The thought of the world where he lived made Guy shudder. People there died for such meaningless reasons most of the time. He stopped the jeep and began to walk south.

Everybody else was walking north. He carried only his camera, which he had not used yet. No one cared that Guy alone was walking south. He stumbled over a corpse of a young child. The young boy must have just died. His mother sat on the burning sand, close to him. She did not cry, she was looking towards the north. She bent down and brushed her lips on the cheek of her dead son. She then rose slowly; and without a backward glance her head held high, she walked north. Guy remembered again that he had not used his camera. A photograph of the mother and dead son would have shaken the world. But would it change anything? He suddenly had a feeling of utter despair. He could do nothing for these people. They would die very soon. Aid from the world would not arrive in time to save the people he walked among now. He had time no desire to take photographs nor to begin describing the horror of the scene in writing.

Guy was still walking south. Night had fallen, and the wind was blowing the sand in Guy's eyes. Some people were still walking, others were sleeping or dying. He lay down on the sand and slept.

The sun rose early the next day and the sand was soon burning hot. Nothing had changed overnight. Many people were dying, but there were still many walking northwards. Everyone was silent. Guy felt a hunger and thirst that he had never experienced before. He felt hot and heavy in his clothes. He looked around and found an abandoned piece of cloth on the sand. It would serve as his clothes from now on. His skin would soon turn black from the sun. He saw no reason to walk south anymore. He had no desire to accomplish his mission. Guy left his camera and clothes lying on the sand and joined the flock of people in a slow shuffle. He could feel like they felt now. They had only one hope, one desire - to stay alive. Guy lifted his head up high and looked straight towards the north as he walked. They were all united in their thoughts, wondering which would come first, food or death.

A note on the Texts

'*The Sea of Yellow Mud*' previously appeared in the privately published collection
'*8 Short Stories*' (2009). '*Cucumber and Mint*' was broadcast on the *BBC World Service* in January 1992.

'*Civil War*' was published in *The Seattle Review Vol xvi, no 2, Fall '93/ Winter '94.*'

Beyond the Horizon' was collected in '*8 Short Stories*'. '*A Sunday in Beirut*' also first appeared in '*8 Short Stories*'. '*Sixteen Years of Dust*' was first published in the *Literary Review, Vol 37, No. 3, Spring 1994*. '*Running on Wind*' appeared in '*Gulf War: Many Perspectives*' published by Virginia Press in 1992. '*Occupation: Photojournalist*' won the student short story prize from the American University of Paris. It appeared in '*8 Short Stories*'.

All the poems quoted as epigraphs can be found in Haas's book '*Beirut Seizures*' (1st edition - *New Earth Publications, Berkley, CA 1993* & 2nd edition – iUniverse 2011).

Glossary

Bekaa Valley – A fertile valley, stretching some 120 kilometres in East Lebanon, between Mount Lebanon to the West and the Anti-Lebanon mountains to the East.

Chtaura – A Lebanese town in the Bekaa Valley, located 44km from Damascus, about halfway on the Beirut to Damascus highway. It is used as a stopping point to rest/eat etc.

Corniche – The seaside promenade in central Beirut.

Katsa – A field intelligence officer of the Mossad.

Kechkaval – A popular cheese in the Lebanon, often imported from Bulgaria.

Khamsin – A dry wind that blows from the south. From the Arabic word for 'fifty' because these windstorms blow sporadically over a period of about fifty days.

Ma'amoul – Small shortbread pastries stuffed with dates, walnuts, pistachios or other fillings.

Markouk – An unleavened flatbread. Village women usually bake it outdoors on an open fire.

Mossad – The national intelligence agency of Israel.

Muezzin – The person appointed at every mosque to lead the call to prayer, traditionally recited five times a day, often now broadcast through a loudspeaker from the top of the minaret.

Oud – A stringed instrument, used in the Middle East similar to the lute, but with a smaller neck and no frets.

Sohat – A Lebanese brand of mineral water.

Ya albi – Affectionate term in Arabic equivalent of my love, sweetheart etc.

Ya Habibi – Male form of Arabic for someone you love.

A Commentary by Joseph Trad

Reading this collection of Haas's eight Short Stories sends me through time to our common history, our happy childhood years in Lebanon, our forced exit from our homeland and then the continuous struggle until adulthood. As I read the stories again, I am struck by a deep sense of 'longing' which seems to permeate every story, binding them together as if they are part of one long novel. This longing is more than just a feeling; it is a cry, a howl that many of Haas's characters utter as they attempt through their aspirations, torments and dreams to transcend their own anguish. It is a call to the readers to believe that life is better when they are in accord with their fellow humans. Life is better when they are able to stand facing their opponents with honesty and truth rather than turning their back to them.

In a sense we all have these moments, a time we all long for. As when his mom sang his favourite song "Que Sera Sera, what will be will be", we all hear in it the echo of an innocent age when life was once good, but the future uncertain. Similarly in "Civil War", the protagonist finds himself in a background reminiscent of Haas: "You stand by the deserted St. George pool and remember the time when you were ten and you and your friends would climb the white-washed walls surrounding the pool..." I can imagine Haas standing there, early on, or later in life on his last visit to his homeland. As if his spirit still lingers there and looks "at the blonde women in bikinis."

The longing motif takes another meaning in "Cucumber and Mint", when the characters become painfully conscious of their forced departure from the homeland. In which city, are these people living, I keep asking myself as I read this story: Beirut, Baghdad, Damascus? As if the world of wars renders us all inhabitants of the same milieu. Haas describes with gentleness and intricate details some moments that urge us to open our hearts to the sheer beauty of living. "The almond tree would soon bloom.... like little specks of soft white clouds ....the almond blossoms will fill the valley...." Tamina, the main character, reminisces on this beauty just a few moments before she is inducted into the registry of "immigrants".

Globe - trotting the world to be with 'people' defying the stereotype of nationals and nationalities, Haas's journeys are nothing but a true longing to show us that people, at the very end, are one with one another once the masks of prejudice and indifference are shed. In "A Sunday in Beirut", the father is bound to his homeland, he needs 'the rush of rockets falling all around'. The son longs for other countries and other lives. This same kind of longing is recaptured in "Occupation: Photojournalist" where Guy's ultimate rejection of his camera where he "left (it) and clothes lying on the sand" only to join "the flock of people in a slow shuffle." It is a symbolic gesture to assert his need not only to capture the real world but also to join and be part of humanity.

Powerful stories always gear our minds toward one of many existential truths: that life and all its vicissitudes are ephemeral. In "Sixteen Years of Dust", Haas creates a series of montages where blood and horror eerily co-mingle with images of Beaujolais, endive and Rocquefort. Haas writes of Mona's death through the voice of a director: "Cut to an extreme close-up the moment the bullet enters Mona's neck....cut back to the sniper....cut to the red VW....blood dripping from the driver's door into the dust."

Is it not the ultimate wish of a writer to control his destiny through the elements of composition, through words and imagery? But even in this story Haas knew that at the very end *Death* cheats all of us and what is left are those longings that make us attune to one another's plight and render us humans at the very end. Still, we do long for the ultimate feeling of getting away, of flying to a zone where the world is at one with the sense of who we are. And this is precisely what Haas has done throughout his entire life, flying to "a new land". It's like a sublime ritual to renew himself again and again. "We fly faster…to a new land," he wrote in "Beyond the Horizon". "It may not be a perfect land, and possibly far from civilised but it is a place where the mind and the body can be free." Was this Hass's ultimate search in life? I can easily vouchsafe an absolute 'Yes'. His was a heart-wrenching cry to people, to friends, to 'Amoulaki' to his mom singing over and over 'Que Sera Sera what will be will be'. Because if Haas's life meant anything, it was that of a "mind and body" awash with creativity, kindness, determination and love. At the very end, Haas's books will always remain a witness to life gone too soon but rich with the longing to be free, yet and again.

Joseph Trad
Oct 2015

Joseph is Haas's lifetime friend. Joseph lives and works in New York City

A Commentary by Sana Chebaro

Haas's poignant and profound collection of stories plunges us into the depths of the Lebanese civil war (1975 to 1991) viewed from different angles and through various lenses. There is the young boy grappling with the idea of war and the accompanying palpable angst and boredom. There is a mother in fear of abandoning her country who yet wants to protect her family from war. There is the tale of a lover's plight and an adolescent's national estrangement. There is a bitter movie film-maker's exploitation of the war, a housewife's exile, a fighter's confusion and the photojournalist's entrapment.

From the outset, the reader senses the catch-22 of Haas's characters as prisoners in their own country, trapped by the ugliness and agony of a hollow war and the soporific nature of their communities. We embark on the tumultuous fear of abandoning one's country, the emotions of dislocation, leaving loved ones, the stigma of a "refugee" - losing one's home, one's childhood, one's precious memories. Starting afresh, starting from scratch.

The narrative is interrupted with the powerful imagery of escape scenes. Haas takes us on a "light fantastic" as we flee with the characters, flee their senseless suffering, the sounds of rockets in their heads, their grief from losing loved ones, whether a treasured pet dog or a parent, a sister, a friend or a lover. We're able for a moment to numb their pain, their haunting dreams, movie-like flashbacks and violent images, to fill their lungs with the freedom of a faraway land.

Yet, Haas's characters never truly sense this comfort and complacency. These lofty images are juxtaposed with feelings of desertion, alienation, discrimination; characters burdened with identity crises and yearning for a place to call home.

Haas's civil war leaves us with a powerful paradox.

Haas's acute sense of human nature is highlighted through a cross-sectional study of relationships. He sensed a young boy's frustration with his single mother, the conflicting national identities of an adolescent boy and his father, and a repressed housewife's disaffection with her husband. The inner-workings of relationships are only magnified and more easily dissected during times of war, exile and assimilation.

While Haas's characters are somehow trapped in a paradox of contradictory imagery, we are led into the sights, smells and tastes of the Mediterranean. We can smell the bars of olive soap, the landscape of fig trees, pine tree forests and almond blossoms. We can almost taste Haas's velvety aniseed and date cakes, eggplants, mint leaves, wild thyme, okra stew, orange blossom lemonade and feel the "humid air mixed with the salty smell of the sea."

Maybe the last word should be left to the last cryptic, chilling story, "Occupation: Photojournalist." Could this be the same "Guy", who in the first story lost his childhood when he fled home with his mother, the same "Guy" who as an adult in the last story yearns to save a starving mother and her child from a desert famine?

Guy's moral hazard can be left to a multitude of interpretations. Although you feel like a foreigner in a strange land, you still share a common humanity. We are all at one with the suffering and the oppressed, we all have a duty of care and a responsibility to end the fighting.

Sana Chebaro
October 2015

Sana is Haas's maternal cousin. To her, Haas is as an older brother. Sana works and lives in London.

an epilogue by Haas's mom

Once upon a time

Once upon a time, there was a little girl who was pure and innocent. She sang, danced and laughed. She was a joy to behold. She was one of five children in a house of many wants and demands. Her physical needs were met but her heart was hungry for love.

She grew up to be a pretty girl and a helping hand. One day she met her lost prince, a jewel amongst them all. She just sighed and fluttered her long eyelashes. He waited in wonder and they were wed in love and magic. They got married under a blanket of stars, with dozens of family and friends wishing them a good life.

It was during their honeymoon that the groom fell sick. She was pregnant. He died soon after.

She gave birth to a healthy boy and gave him his father's name. She kept to herself for years and decades. She nurtured her child on her own in peace and care and vowed never to marry again. She always remembered the father with honor and respect.

Mother and child were a happy family of two. They were contented in their home together. She went to work. He went to school. Family and friends came to visit every now and then. Serenity filled the house, harmony and devotion was their way. They did not have much to live on but they managed. They felt secured in their home, for the love between them was their bond.

Then one night when all was quiet and calm, they were startled by the sound of an explosion. Dust was everywhere. He woke up crying; they spent the night in the shelters. The next night there was another explosion and a third. The blasts and the damage were getting closer and closer. Night after night they were seeking refuge somewhere. Dust filled the air and gunpowder smoke filled their lungs.

Mother and child bundled a few of their belongings and walked many miles to reach the borders. They never looked back; they never came back. They did not live happily ever after for there was a block in their throats from leaving home. They were refugees and were never safe again. They lived thousands of miles apart and both were far away from their home. There were many separations between mother and child in order to cope and survive. When they came together, they found delight in spite of their bleeding scars.

Mother travelled the world to help the sick and the old. She went wherever there was war. There were many struggles for them both, until the son became an adult and started building his own life. She visited him whenever she could. And when she was in poor health, he nursed her with tenderness and care.

He was his father's son. He was gentle with the oppressed and compassionate with the elderly and the very young. She saw her son worthy of his father's name. She waited patiently; she loved unconditionally; she gave her son everything she had but there was little love left in her heart.

The son looked like his father. He was handsome, fit and with lots of gifts to give. He cherished life and his soul was satisfied. Mother often looked with wonder at her wonderful son and thanked the Divine for the rewards bestowed after all the suffering and the pain.

The son became a writer and resided in tranquillity in a cabin on the top of the mountains. He wrote and wrote. For weeks and years he wrote. He wrote sad stories never told and wrote poems that cried with concern for all. He did not stop writing. He wrote about the devastating war, about the hate and anger that divides people and keeps families apart. He wrote about his fate, his excruciating pain and the many friends and family he would never see again. He wanted to tell the world that war was just like dust. Nothing comes out of it except loss of lives and twisted minds.

He wrote about his mother's friend who disappeared one day during the early days of the war. He never again saw her two children.

Mary Rose*

> *If only I could go back*
> *no more a child*
> *and hold Paul and Rima tight*
> *their pyjamas still damp from their bath*
> *and wait with them. A cup of sweet, warm milk*
> *and they sleep and never dream of Mary Rose*
> *their mother*
> *four pieces under a bridge.*

He wrote about his fatherless classmate whose mother was shot and killed at night in the elevator of their home.

While Hadi sleeps*

> *One. Two. Three shots.*
> *Blood drips from the elevator door.*
> *Upstairs, Hadi turns over and sleeps*
> *on his stomach, breathing lightly into his pillow,*
> *waiting for his mother's damp breath*
> *to warm the back of his neck.*

He wrote about the opera singer who lived next door. A sniper killed him while playing his piano at home.

They shot the piano player*

> *And across the alley*
> *his fingers were fondling,*

stroking the thin ivory blades
while music rose
from the pirouetting curtains
in the Levantine breeze.
Sirens in the dark alley.
A corpse in a black plastic bag,
his mother pulling him away from the window
the wicked breeze
wicked she said.

He wrote and wrote until one day he could write no more. He got up in the morning and for no reason at all he put all his writings in his only suitcase and said he was heading home. After 25 years he was going home. His mother, too frail to make the trip, blessed her son and bid him farewell.

In his childhood home, where his father died and he was born, he found his love and lots of joy. For no reason at all, one afternoon, he bent his head on the sofa at home. 'I am a little tired' he said.

Later, a call came for the mother echoing a deep hollow sound:

'Come identify the body'.
'Come identify the body'.
'Come identify the body'.

The son was buried in the cradle of his father's bones.

Haas's mom
Oct 2015

---

* *Haas Mroue*, **Beirut Seizures**, (1st edition - *New Earth Publications, Berkley, CA 1993 &* 2nd edition – iUniverse 2011).

Context: The Lebanese Civil War

Civil War ravaged Lebanon for fifteen years and six months between 1975 and 1991 and resulted in years of political and social instability.

The origins of the war are complex and hard to trace, as they are with any war but particularly in a country with such a diverse population and history of occupation and persecution.

Lebanon is still deeply wounded by its civil war. It is estimated that around 150,000 people were killed and another 100,000 permanently handicapped by injuries. Approximately 900,000 people, a fifth of the pre-war population, were displaced from their homes. And a quarter of a million fled the country permanently.

A more detailed overview of the conflict can be found on the <u>Lebanese Civil War page on Wikipedia</u>, which includes a list of resources and further reading.

Printed in the United States
By Bookmasters